Early Praise for
Executive Roadkill

"Unfortunately, anyone that has worked in corporate America could identify with the characters and/or the situation in this book. Your situation may not have gone quite as far as the one in Executive Roadkill, but you will recognize it. This was an easy read that kept me entertained and wondering what was going to happen next."
-Brad Myers, PGA Golf Professional, Author

"Just finished the book, and the take-away was stunning. Anyone of us, in business, could easily find ourselves in the same position as the character in Sisti's book. How often have we made decisions without the benefit of hindsight that could have left us vulnerable to being "thrown under the bus", or worse. Well worth the read."
-Thomas C. Mulvihill, Author, Entrepreneur

"Think you had a bad day at the office? In "Executive Roadkill" author Michael Sisti takes you on a horrifying yet humorous journey to corporate hell and back. He takes office politics to a whole new level of bad. A really good read about really bad stuff!"
-L.S.

"It is a complicated story with self-biographic touch. The narrative style is emphasizing how serious the conflicts are in the corporate world behind the curtains."
-Lajos Hajdu

"I received this book 2 days ago and could not stop reading it. It depicted the everyday goings on in any major company in New England. It gives insight to the real thought processes of executives and how there are many sides to stories. One thing for sure is that there are still hard-working dedicated people in companies and the truth always comes out."
-Anonymous

"An inside look at corporate America and the way things are done. I enjoyed this book even though I have been out of the corporate world for a few years. There are lessons to be learned and taken to heart. I am sure many readers will be familiar with the premise and fallout."
-Mary Nickell

"Great read that never ceases to amaze throughout the story. Cleverly depicts how power can turn ugly in the corporate world."
-Jo Ellen Grossman

"A fast-moving eyeopener into the corporate world. Believable characters that reveal themselves as the book unfolds."
-Susan Turner

EXECUTIVE ROADKILL

MICHAEL A. SISTI

OH!
ORSINI
HOUSE

Executive Roadkill

by Michael A. Sisti

© Copyright 2024 Michael A. Sisti

This is a work of fiction.
All the characters in this book are fictitious,
and any resemblance to actual persons, living or dead,
is purely coincidental. The names, incidents, dialogue,
and opinions expressed are products
of the author's imagination and
are not to be construed as real.

Published by

Bradenton, FL 34203
www.michaelsisti.com

This book is dedicated to
the incredibly talented staff that worked
for me during those tumultuous days
described in this novel.
And also to the team of creative,
production, and account service
professionals at our advertising agency.
Together you enabled me
to achieve the height of success
during my career.

**The story told in this novel is based
on actual events. Only the names have been
changed to protect the ignorant, innocent,
and the bystanders.**

Hubris

Hubris, pronounced "hugh-bris," is a great word. If you look it up in the dictionary, you'll see something like "excessive pride or arrogance" and perhaps learn of its use in classic Greek tragedies where ruthless ambition and disregard of the limits that govern human actions lead to the hero's downfall. People with hubris make up their own rules and spin convention to fit their personal needs.

I see it all the time, mostly from businesspeople, academics, and politicians jockeying for the top rung, or from those who have made it to the top and wait impatiently for the coronation to begin.

They look out over all their conquered lands, mystified that the unwashed masses are not bowing in solemn adulation or cowering in the presence of their brilliance.

There are, of course, wonderful men and women who achieve both happiness and material success while maintaining perspective and respect for others. They're just hard to spot because they keep a low profile and share the limelight. They are too busy enjoying the intangible moments to grab the bullhorn and make public announcements.

(Excerpted with permission from Moments . . . Not Years by Michael Hayes Samuelson)

Prologue

It was well after nine o'clock on a slow Monday evening and all the guests at Capriccio's had completed their dinners and left the landmark restaurant in downtown Providence. The dimly lit, low ceiling, yet elegant environment was favored by couples seeking romantic interlude and businesspeople preferring anonymity. Two men wearing suits and ties arrived within minutes of each other, shook hands and took a table in a far corner of the large dining room.

After ordering martinis, Jack, with a self-assured air of success sipped his drink while flicking a speck of dust from the sleeve of his tailored suit. He was well proportioned for a man in his late forties, and good looking, with greying hair and dark penetrating eyes. He said to his companion, "Phil, you look like shit. What's wrong?"

Hesitating before his vacant eyes lifted, the gaunt, white-haired gentleman said, "Jack, I'm in big trouble and I need your help. The world has passed me by. Twenty years ago, I was the most powerful man in Rhode Island. Now I have almost no clients, and I'm burning through my savings."

Surprised by the appearance of his companion who wore a rumpled, ill-fitting suit and looked older than is age, Jack scowled, "So, what do you want me to do about it? What about your law practice and your lobbying business? You always had such enviable clients."

Before answering, he slurped a second gulp of his martini. "When I left the legislature, everyone owed me, and that's how I built my client base. As the favors ran out, so did the clients. Let's face it, I never understood law well enough to practice it. I'm a dealmaker, a behind-the-scenes fixer. And by the time I shifted to lobbying, almost all my contacts in the state government were retired and gone. So, I hate to admit it, but I've become useless."

"It sure sounds like you're in a jam. What are you going to do about it?"

"I was just hired by RIHIP. The problem is I got the job by convincing them they needed me to keep the legislature at bay. But honestly, Jack, I don't think I can perform up to their needs. And quite frankly, I don't think there is any threat from the state."

"No, there isn't, but you landed yourself a plum position. How did you pull it off?"

"It's no secret the company is in decline and may never return to its glory days. I told them about how Vermont took over Blue Cross in their state and how the same thing could happen to them here, particularly since they are losing so much money."

"That's a good ploy. You must have scared them."

"Oh, I did. One of the top executives there is a golf buddy of mine. We both belong to the same club. He stepped up and helped convince the CEO that I'm the guy who can get the legislature to help bail out the company." Phil sat there hunched over and took a huge swig of his drink before continuing. "The problem is that I'm not up for the role. And I'm terrified. If I can't perform, I'll get fired."

"Look Phil, this is a sweet opportunity, and you have me on your side. I can make it work for you. It's all about the money. As soon as you get settled into the job, you start building up their PAC budget to about two mil. Then get me in there to do a couple of business deals.

"I'll spread lots of money around and make sure you have the full support of the legislature. And I will make you look like a hero at RIHIP. Now, relax and let me guide you. Get me in the door and you and I will both make a ton of money!"

Chapter 1

Immobility in Action

When Dave Powers drove from his custom-built home early that morning, he was focused on the upcoming needs analysis. The trek to Rhode Island was the first step of an assignment at Rhode Island Health Insurance Partners. The project came at the invitation of his wife Elisa's friend, Joan Rotino, the insurer's executive vice president. RIHIP, as the company was known, had lost $25 million the previous year, and was projected to lose a similar amount in the current year.

Joan had been hired to take over the firm's sales and marketing division and return the company as the premiere insurer in the state. For years they had dominated the market, reaching 85% share. But in a few short years, that had fallen to 49% and dropping.

Over the previous ten months, they had listened to Joan's outlandish stories about the company on her frequent calls to Elisa. Knowing her penchant for embellishing her lavish narratives, they accepted her ruminations with a five-pound grain of iodized salt. But

Dave knew there had to be some substance behind her outlandish reporting.

Arriving at RIHIP's office campus shortly before nine, Joan greeted him and introduced him to her assistant, Marie who would accompany him throughout the day.

Dave was average height with a trim build, a constant smile, and a self-confident, take-charge presence. Brown wavy hair and dark-rimmed glasses accented his twinkling brown eyes.

Marie brought him to a series of meetings taking place throughout the organization, where he sat silently hour after hour listening to the diatribe. In each case, the solution to the perceived problem seemed so obvious that he assumed there were factors he wasn't aware of.

During the meeting immediately after lunch, the group in the conference room was flummoxed by the fact that very few Medicare subscribers were responding to a recent mailing regarding diabetes issues. Everyone in the room was stymied as no one could come up with a solution.

With the *Italian Grinda* attacking his digestive system, Dave was exasperated and couldn't sit there any longer. The simple answer was staring them in the face. He blurted out, "Why don't you send an urgent follow-up email as a reminder to everyone who didn't respond? Maybe an email will get their attention."

The reaction was stone silence making Dave nervous. When no one commented on his idea, the moderator finally broke the silence and said, "Well, we've never done that before."

Incredulously, Dave shot back, "Don't you ever try anything new? Other companies do this all the time." The body language in the room changed noticeably and spoke volumes as everyone shrank back and stiffened in the chilling air.

At that point, the moderator broke up the meeting, scheduling another one for the following week. One of the attendees walked up to Dave and asked, "Yaw not from around here, ah ya?"

He jokingly replied, "No. Why? Did you have trouble understanding my broken Brooklynese?"

Instead of a smile, Dave got a sneer as the executive turned and left.

Chapter 2

The Problem is Us

At the end of the day, Dave met with Joan who was bubbling over with enthusiasm. Joan was an overweight woman with a beautiful round face that emphasized her Italian heritage. She had dark hair, expressive black eyes, and a warm welcoming smile. "So, how did it go?"

Dave dropped into a chair and hung his head. "Not well at all. Joan, you've got to rethink your plans. These people don't just dislike change, they are scared to death of it."

"I certainly agree that they are not action-oriented."

"Actually, they're comatose. There's no way they're going to cooperate with a major restructure to the market-driven approach you're proposing."

"Listen to me. You write the plan, and I'll make it happen."

"Joan, I'm always up for a challenge and I look forward to this opportunity, but I'm convinced that if you try to force this change, you will simply paralyze them with fear. And your budding career at RIHIP will end in failure before you even get out of the chute."

"I agree with your assessment. I've been facing it since I got here. But here's the kicker. Our CEO, Al Conover has our full support and is committed to it. I've already restructured the sales department, bringing in a broker network. The sales team was very angry at that development. But sales are increasing dramatically."

Dave nodded. "Having the CEO's backing will make a big difference. The challenge is the people who refuse to accept change. I can see a wholesale layoff coming."

Laughing, Joan answered, "That's not going to happen. At this company, the only way an employee gets terminated is for murder or rape, and in most cases, they have to commit both with heinous intent."

"Okay, I'm jumping ahead. We know the problem, and we will deal with it. I'll be back next week to take a hard look at the communications process, and then I'll make my report."

Driving home that evening, Dave thought about his surreal day. *I attended five meetings, and they were all the same. People droned on for an hour without saying anything but loved to hear themselves speak. Nothing was accomplished except to schedule another useless meeting. It was the worst case of stone-age bureaucracy I have ever encountered. I can't wait to get home and tell Elisa that all of Joan's horror stories were actually true.*

Chapter 3

Survival Plan

Following a week of interviews with the advertising agency, all the directors in Joan's division, plus the AVP and everyone in the communications department, Dave was exhausted. Returning to his home office in Ramsey, NJ, he shared his notes with Elisa, explained the barriers he encountered, and asked for her input. He wrote a very strong recommendation and proposal for his firm to take over the RIHIP's marketing communications function under his direction for two years.

Returning to Providence the following week, after Joan and Al Conover's review of the document, he presented it to the entire Senior Staff. With Al's blessing, the proposal was accepted unanimously. After the meeting Al asked Dave if he could start within two weeks. Dave answered, "I'll be ready."

Excited to launch this two-year consulting engagement, Dave savored the challenge. RIHIP was a burgeoning bureaucracy of 2,000 employees. For most of them it was the only job they ever had, and they all expected to retire from there at the end of their career.

16

He was relishing the idea of shaking them up and making them more responsive and productive.

But he was dreading the first steps in restructuring the Marketing Communications Department. One third of the twenty-member staff were at manager or director level, and none had the skills to handle themselves, much less their reports. The department's AVP had been fired after Dave uncovered an arrangement that he had with the ad agency to provide him season tickets to the Providence Bruins hockey games, among other perks. The agency was also terminated.

Dave's contract was to reorganize the department, motivate the staff, improve productivity, and deliver an impactful message to their constituencies. All this with the expectancy of returning the company to its lofty position as the dominant health insurer in Rhode Island.

As he began to flatten out and restructure his department, the non-performers, which were two thirds of the staff, quickly fled the company. These slackers had no tolerance for change, lacked ambition and creativity, and only cherished their titles and their cushy jobs. Faced with the task of having to earn their salaries, they trampled over each other as they stampeded out the door. The mass exit turned out to be the best development that could happen at this early stage. Dave could now build a quality team from scratch.

He was fortunate to interview and hire Donna Marino for the director position of the department. She was in her forties, full figured, with a charming, dimpled face. Her designer glasses drew attention to her beautiful blue eyes. Donna had a large network of Rhode Island-based contacts that included many talented people with creative skills who jumped at the chance to join the company and work under her.

At a reorganizational meeting held in their large conference room, Dave explained his philosophy of building a creative-driven staff that would produce innovative marketing programs and outstanding communications material. He explained, "Mundane and dull are not in my vocabulary." And then he added, "We are going to adopt the philosophy of Company SEX." Seeing the horrified look on everyone's faces before he could continue, his smirk relaxed them as he clarified, "Strategy, Execution, Xceptionalism."

During this orientation, he advised them that if they considered this a job where the only motivation was a salary, then they should quit and find other work. He wanted them to look forward to coming to the office every day, because it was a career opportunity to learn, grow, and succeed. "If you want to be in an environment where you get to enjoy the opportunity to introduce new ideas, this is it. And, believe me, I will make it fun every day. I look for humor in everything that happens around me. It's how I sharpen my own creative skills. And I want you to do the same. Within a couple of months, people will be begging to work in our little Utopia."

Dave then asked each member of the reorganized department to introduce themselves, their role and a little about their background. Last to speak was Dave himself, and he explained his task as a branding and marketing consultant hired to restructure and run the department. He told them about his agency in New Jersey and how he would be traveling back and forth, overseeing two operations.

He further advised them that the new Marketing Communications department would be run more like an advertising agency rather than a typical corporate department. They would be serving the company's executives and staff as internal clients. He ended by sharing his lingering apprehension at functioning effectively within a corporate bureaucracy. He explained that he was a serial entrepreneur and that mindset conflicted with corporate culture. One of the graphic designers, Marylou Prior asked, "What's a serial entrepreneur?"

Dave responded, "That's someone who packages corn flakes for a living."

As the meeting broke up with everyone smiling and realizing that this would be no normal tour of duty. They all left the conference room elated and anticipating the adventures that lay ahead.

Chapter 4

Tilting at Silos

Dave's production manager, Denise Moran placed the printed sample on his desk. "Dave, this new brochure is a mess. It's so poorly printed that it would be an embarrassment to distribute it."

He examined it and looked up at her. "You're right. This is unacceptable. The last few print orders have been awful. Reject this shipment, and have the printer rerun it at his own expense. Maybe that will get their attention."

Dave had now been consulting for RIHIP for six months and was just getting comfortable in the position. Denise was one of the new members of the team that Donna brought in. She was a steadfast production manager with many years of experience in both the ad agency environment, as well as in corporate settings. And her response resonated that background.

"It's not that easy, Dave. First of all, we must go through the print manager in the purchasing department. Technically, it's his call. And second, the printer is one of our health insurance customers. This is RIHIP, and you can't overlook the politics of these situations. Purchasing protects that relationship, so delivering sloppy work tends to be the norm around here."

He quickly countered, "Well, that cozy mindset is unacceptable. We must have excellent quality on all our material. Our brand demands it. Running our department under these terms is like going to war with bureaucratic rules of engagement."

Smiling, she answered, "Well, we do work for a bureaucracy, if you haven't noticed."

"Don't remind me. We've got to be able to make unencumbered decisions without taking every vendor and every employee's concern into consideration."

And after thinking for a minute, he added, "OK, then handle it this way. Call the printer in and tell him to come to our office because we want his advice on some technical issues. When he gets here, show him the problem, and ask him why this happened and how we can avoid it in the future. After that, I will call Lawrence in purchasing, explain the steps we took without him, and work out a compromise on how we manage our printing orders going forward."

"Lawrence and the entire department will freak out when you call in the printer directly without going through them."

The next morning the owner of the printing company came into the office with the expectation of demonstrating his vast knowledge of print production. He was also certain someone from Purchasing would be at the meeting. Denise brought him into Dave's office and introduced him. "Dave, this is Tim Spears from Cranston Litho."

Shaking hands, Dave smiled, and after a few minutes of asking about his equipment, services, and staff, he handed the Tim a sample of the brochure.

"How would you rate the quality of this brochure?" Dave asked.

Before answering, he inquired, "Is Lawrence or anyone from Purchasing going to be in the meeting?"

"We didn't ask any of them to be here. I thought you and I could discuss this printing project and I could also learn more about your capabilities."

"This is highly unusual. I think someone from upstairs should be here. After all, they write the purchase orders."

Dave asked Denise to call Lawrence and have him come down and join the meeting. When Lawrence came down, he was surprised and annoyed to see the printer, but held his tongue to see what was going on.

Dave explained why he called in the printer. "We're just getting started, so let me ask my questions, and you can participate in the discussion, and afterwards, we can meet separately and talk about any remaining issues."

Dave again asked Tim to examine the printed sample and comment on it. Scanning the document, the printer responded, "It looks pretty good, although the quality of the photos appears to be sub-par. Are you having trouble with your photographer?"

Reaching into his top desk drawer, Dave pulled out a printer's magnifying loupe and studied the printing on the pages of the brochure. He then handed the loupe and the printed flyer to Tim and had him look at the magnified ink pattern. "Take a look at the dot structure and the ink coverage and tell me you still think the problem is the photography we supplied. I know my dots, and your dots are not good dots."

The printer, realizing that Dave had intimate knowledge of the printing process, had no response for the poorly printed material. He had a sheepish look on his face and shrugged his shoulders. So, with that opening Dave told him, "Here's your options. You can walk away without admitting to the inferior quality of the work, and we'll pay for the printing. But we will not give you any more orders that require superior quality. Or you can reprint the brochures at your expense, and assuming you can demonstrate that you can meet our quality expectations, we will use our flexibility to request your services on a larger share of the print work we buy. Which way do you want to go?"

Before the printer could respond, Dave sensing the tension from Lawrence, turned and asked him, "Are you okay with my solution?"

"Under the circumstances, I am. But let's discuss this privately after this meeting."

"Agreed." And turning to the printer, Dave nodded.

"Dave, you obviously know the printing process, and you're imminently fair. We have the latest digital upgrades on our equipment, and a top-flight production team. We can meet and exceed your expectations. I apologize for coming up short on this project, but we will reprint it to your satisfaction, and will earn your trust as your go-to printer for the most demanding jobs."

That was the answer Dave was looking for. And he commented to the printer, "That's the attitude I was hoping for. And I'll be counting on you to perform. Because if things don't work out here and I get fired, I may have to come to you for a job running a press."

The comment caught the printer by surprise, until he saw the smirk on Dave's face.

When the printer left, Dave brought Lawrence into his office. As soon as the door closed, a very angry Lawrence asked, "What the hell are you doing? These are my decisions to make. You can't infringe on my responsibility."

Expecting this reaction, he explained, "I went directly to the vendor because the system isn't working. Your team simply doesn't have the knowledge of the printing process that I have, and they really don't know how to determine acceptable quality."

"That doesn't excuse you overstepping your bounds, and it pisses me off."

"Lawrence, I'm not your enemy, I want to be your friend and work together." Before he could respond, Dave suggested that they talk at lunch and work it out. The suggestion defused the situation.

Chapter 5

Inside the Silo

The two men walked to Zapata's, a tiny Mexican restaurant that did wonders with eggplant, a rather unusual vegetable for this type of cuisine. Dave thought he had a good relationship with Lawrence based on when he evaluated the company's in-house printing and warehousing operation.

Dave's recommendations gave Lawrence more control over the combined departments. Knowing how territorial all the managers at RIHIP were, he hoped to use this favor in order to get Lawrence to accept the recommendation he was about to make. He also knew that he had to sweeten the deal to get it done.

They quickly ordered and Dave got right to the point. "Lawrence, I have two issues to discuss with you. I want to find a way that we can put more work into your in-house operation." This grabbed Lawrence's attention. Dave continued, "We also need to adjust the procurement process to achieve better quality. The printed material has been substandard. My department needs more control over the quality."

"I'm sorry to hear that, Dave. Why didn't you call me? I'm sure I could have easily resolved this issue. And if necessary, I have a way to step on their nuts without them losing their ability to make babies."

Dave took a moment to collect his thoughts. "Look, I'm not looking to go to war with the vendors. We can't always be buying the low-bid printing without taking value into consideration. It's reflecting on our brand image. People sub-consciously equate a sparkling brochure with a superior product.

"So, here's what I'm thinking. I want you to put in a requisition for a new 29" printing press, and I will write a memo supporting your request. We are designing a new format for all our product flyers, and with that press, your department will be able to efficiently produce the entire series."

Lawrence nodded. "I'm liking this. Keep going."

"For the large volume color brochures and other printing that doesn't fit your equipment, I want Marketing Communications to select the printers and provide a rationale for our selected printer if they're not the low bidder. You will prepare the PO, approve the invoice, and confirm the printed quantity when the order is placed in inventory. So, there's never any opportunity for fraud. We will just approve the quality. This will meet all the corporate regs and controls, and we get the quality we require. And what do you think?"

Lawrence paused, savoring his eggplant. "You've obviously thought this through, and it does cover all the bases. However, I'm not sure we can get the purchasing AVP to sign off on it. This is a major shift in procedure, not always using the low bidder. But I will support your recommendation, and I am delighted that you are willing to back me on the request for the new press. I have felt for a long time that we need that size to increase our productivity. And with you designing the flyers to fit the press, we should have no problem getting the req okayed."

Driving home that afternoon, Dave reflected on his day, and felt good about the way he handled the situation and his growing comfort level in navigating the corporate maze.

When I got here, I could not understand the structure where every department was a silo, and each manager jealously protected his turf. I'm still wondering how a corporate bureaucracy can be productive and efficient. The money being wasted is staggering.

Chapter 6

Blondes at the Baby Shower

Returning from a working lunch meeting with Joan and the CEO in his office, Dave found a group email to his staff.

From   Kim Venable
To   MarComm Mail Group
Subject Baby Shower

Thank you all so much for the surprise baby shower. Your generosity and thoughtfulness are overwhelming. The gift certificate will definitely come in handy. The pizza was great, and the dessert was better. I loved the cake, but my favorite was the brownies and the blondes.

Thanks again

From   Dave Powers
To   Kim Venable
Cc   MarComm Mail Group
Subject Re: Baby Shower

Blondes? There were blondes at the party? Why didn't someone tell me? I would have canceled my meeting with Joan and been there.

From	Lee Chang
To	Dave Powers
Cc	MarComm Mail Group
Subject	Re: Baby Shower

Dave, you like blondes? In China, all my cousins are blonde.

From	Dave Powers
To	Lee Chang
Cc	MarComm Mail Group
Subject	Re: Baby Shower

If your cousins in China are all blonde, they are spending too much time in the sun.

Chapter 7

Opening the Silo

Two days later, a meeting was held in Purchasing's conference room. Fred Snyder, the AVP of Purchasing led the session. Lawrence brought in his print department and warehouse managers, and Dave came upstairs with his production manager, Denise and her assistant, Gail Goldberg. Dave explained the quality control issue and shared his recommendations for the modifications to the purchase process. At first, Snyder expressed that he was comfortable with the controls that were in place and saw no reason to change them.

Expecting his resistance to even this small incursion into his department, Dave turned to Lawrence and spoke up. "Fred, this issue is real. Not only are we getting unsatisfactory printing, but we're also creating tension with some of the printers who are also our corporate clients. I've already received a call from one of our sales reps expressing concern for his customer. We don't want any of these vendors leaving RIHIP for another insurer over a disagreement about quality. I strongly endorse Dave's proposal, and I think we should implement it immediately."

Fred looked over the proposal. "Let me read this and have my staff review it. I'll have an answer for you this week. Vendors also being customers certainly complicates the issue in your favor. I want to do the right thing, but I don't want to antagonize them"

By the end of the week, the directive came down from Purchasing with the recommended modifications. That same day, Dave got an email from Lawrence, congratulating him on getting the change implemented, and asking him to write the memo supporting his request to purchase the new printing press.

Within a two-month period, the press was delivered, and set up for operation. The entire episode gave Dave a sense that with the right approach, progress and change at less than glacial speed was possible in a burgeoning corporate entity. Now all he had to do was get the managers to think like entrepreneurs, another seemingly insurmountable task.

Chapter 8

Welcome to Wellness

Making RIHIP's subscribers healthier was the best way to keep insurance premiums down. To achieve that, the company was developing a wellness program to corporate and group clients. And if claims improved at these companies, their premiums would go down.

The director of this program called Dave and asked about an announcement program to publicize the effort. Dave suggested that he or someone from his department attend a Marketing Communications weekly meeting and as the internal client, present the program to the communications staff.

At the next team meeting, a nerdy woman joined the group. Her name was Felicia Myerson. She explained that she had a PhD in nutrition, and she just exuded health. Her tight, dark pants suit emphasized an impressive trim body. However, her severe look, with her hair pulled tight in a bun and her dark, thick-framed glasses. Dave was convinced that if she smiled, her face would shatter like a falling wine glass.

Ms. Myerson, as she liked to be called, opened her presentation with a question, "Do any of you know what Free Radicals are?"

Before anyone could respond, Dave answered, "Yes, they are Bernie Sanders followers."

Everyone laughed except Ms. Myerson, who turned beet-red and struggled to contain her composure. Unfortunately, Dave didn't get to see if her face would shatter.

Following the presentation, Dave assigned two staff members to develop a campaign to communicate the wellness program to the RIHIP members. When their concept was complete, he wanted them to present their ideas to the entire department and get everyone's feedback before finalizing the program.

An Offer He Couldn't Refuse

CEO Al Conover had been pressuring Dave to take a full-time position with the company, pushing hard to get him to change his status from an outside consultant to Chief Communications Officer by joining the firm. Sitting in Al's office, the two of them were discussing the issue.

Al said, "Dave, everyone is impressed with what you accomplished in such a short time. It's making me realize that I need you here full-time. Your part-time consulting is not giving the company the full benefit of your services."

"But you can't afford me full-time. My agency provides more income than Joan Rotino makes and she's an EVP."

Discussing Al's offer left Dave with lingering but diminishing concerns about working for a large bureaucracy. He'd never done before, and the move would drop his income exponentially. However, his wife Elisa had just been recently diagnosed with breast cancer and feared losing her health insurance in the future. Elisa was less troubled by the pay drop because she preferred the peace of mind that came with the company's generous benefits package.

A lifelong entrepreneur, Dave never even considered working for a large corporation. He always referred to it as *going over to the Dark Side.* However, the consulting gig at this 2,000-employee bureaucracy turned out to be an excellent opportunity to learn to adjust from his freewheeling entrepreneurial mindset to this radically different, analytical corporate culture.

Before Al could respond to Dave's concern about compensation, Dick Nichols walked into Al's office. Dick was one of the company's executive vice-presidents and would probably become CEO whenever Al decided to retire. Tall, well-built, brown wavy hair and hazel eyes, his movie-star looks had all the women fantasizing over him.

Al introduced Dick as he sat in the chair next to Dave. "Welcome to RIHIP. We haven't had a chance to meet as I've been extremely busy. Do you play golf?"

"Whenever I can," said Dave, "which isn't often enough."

"Great, we'll get together very soon and play a round."

Al interrupted Dick and said, "I'm glad you came in. I've been trying to convince Dave to come onboard full-time. We need his complete attention to help us regain our position in the Rhode Island market."

Turning to Dave, Al said, "I get that you're concerned about compensation. And given our losses, I can't pay you what you're worth right now. But if you take the position I'm offering, you will get a huge benefits package that you would have a hard time funding at your agency. At the rate we're going on this recovery, within two years, I can elevate you to a vice president position and give you a substantial bump in pay. And with all the perks and benefits you'll make almost as much here with less work than running your business."

With Conover giving Dave unprecedented latitude to make his own decisions, this was becoming a dream job. However, every once in a while, a situation like the recent printing problem, gave him pause for concern. But with some creative maneuvering, he was learning how to get his way without making waves. And if Elisa could generate some income in Rhode Island, they probably could achieve parity with their current compensation.

Chapter 10

The Ghost

Dave got to the office one morning at his usual time of six in the morning, and about an hour later someone was standing in his doorway. An even bigger surprise than having a visitor so early without an appointment, was that it was Phil Lyons, a recluse who almost never ventured out of his office. In fact, he was referred to as *The Ghost*. His pale complexion and white hair further contributed to the moniker. He almost never came to the office and rarely attended staff meetings.

Lyons spent nearly all his time up at the statehouse lobbying for the firm's insurance concerns. Whenever he was seen at the company's headquarters, he was following Dick Nichols around like a little puppy dog waiting for his Milkbone treat.

Lyons was the Vice President Legislative Affairs. Before joining the company, he had been a practicing attorney in Providence, and had served as Senate Majority Leader in the legislature for nearly twenty years. Despite this long-term leadership position, he did not project a commanding presence. His body language said otherwise. Phil was an underweight, frail individual with stooped, rounded shoulders, and he always seemed to have a frightened look on his face with his eyes shifting left and right.

Dave couldn't resist making a comment, "Phil, you startled me. I thought it was a ghost standing there. Come on in and sit down." Without any greeting or small talk, Lyons, leaning against the doorjamb shared the reason for his visit. "I wanted to let you know that House Speaker, Jacques Landrieu will be calling you for an appointment. He wants to present a marketing opportunity involving the independent pharmacies in Rhode Island.

Lyons went on to explain that RIHIP had an adversarial relationship with the Independent Pharmacy Association in Rhode Island due to its provider network structure. The independent pharmacies were excluded from the HMO networks as a way to reduce costs, as they could not afford to offer the discounts available from the national chains such as CVS, Walgreens, etc. Because of this exclusion, the pharmacy association constantly lobbied for legislation to force RIHIP to include them in all their networks.

Before he left, Lyons also asked about buying promotional gifts that he could give out to legislators and people who worked for the state agencies and government. Dave explained the complex new procurement process to him, and that his department could handle that purchasing for him.

Lyons said, "I want to make my own purchases, so I can use these opportunities with my own contacts to generate favors from time to time."

Dave said he had no problem with Lyons doing his own ordering on these small purchases, as long as he stayed within the protocol. He suggested to Phil that he process the paperwork through Denise and have the orders delivered to the warehouse to expedite payment. Lyons agreed to follow the process.

Chapter 11

The Bag Man

After Lyons left, Dave wondered about his unusual behavior. He was very puzzled by this executive's strange behavior.

Lyons is rarely seen on the campus and had almost no contact with any of the company's staff. So why had he bothered to come to my office? He had already sent an email about Landrieu's request. And the email contained all the pharmacy information that Lyons just explained. And why did he really want to do his own ordering of merchandise, particularly after I explained the convoluted purchasing process which is a clerical headache. It's not adding up.

A couple of weeks later, Landrieu came to Dave's office to make his presentation. Accompanying him was his associate, Steve Fisher. Seeing that the business card holder on Powers' desk was a replica of the famous seventh hole at Pebble Beach, he immediately established a rapport around golf. He offered to have Dave as his guest at Kirkbrae Country Club, where he was a member.

After accepting cups of coffee, the trio sat at the small conference table, where Landrieu explained the situation with the pharmacies, and his task of preventing legislation that would be harmful to RIHIP. He offered a solution that really caught Dave's attention. Like most of the part-time legislators in Rhode Island, Jack, as he liked to be called, supported himself by running a business.

His company purchased pharmacy prescription bags by the tens of millions that he distributed free to all the pharmacies within each of the national chains, saving them millions of dollars a year. The bags carried advertising for the pharmaceutical manufacturers' products, including brands like Crestor, Humira, Pravachol, etc. The cost of the advertising covered the expense of producing and distributing the bags and gave Jack a nice profit.

The independent pharmacies, due to their much smaller volumes, did not participate in this program, so they had to purchase their own prescription bags which are costly to them. And here was the opportunity for RIHIP. Landrieu was offering a program where he would produce bags in quantities of one million with RIHIP's health insurance products promoted on them. He explained that he could print that quantity, warehouse them at the bag manufacturer, and drop ship them as needed to each pharmacy in the state. The pharmacists would welcome the savings, and more importantly, would appreciate the idea that RIHIP was partnering with them in its promotions. He said, "It's a clean, hands-free promotion that's cost-effective and will improve your standing with the independent pharmacies."

Dave recognized the strength of the proposal and told him he'd get back to him within a week. Before leaving, the two men each gave Dave their cards. Jack explained that if the company wanted to move ahead, to contact Fisher, who handled all of the day-to-day management of the company, particularly when the legislature was in session.

After they left his office, Dave called Wendy Ketler. She was the EVP of the Medicare Division, who also ran the Provider Relations Department that included the pharmacy networks. When he explained the program, she was thrilled, particularly when he suggested that they could promote the new Medicare product on the bags. Recognizing that the retiree segment of the population was the biggest, most loyal customer base of the independent pharmacies, she said that this was a winning marketing and public relations coup that benefitted both her divisions. "Dave, you never cease to amaze!"

Chapter 12

The Ticket Giveaway

Because of RIHIP's sponsorships and advertising throughout the state, Dave often got perks and complementary tickets to events. Most of the time, he handed them off to the sales department for the reps to use to entertain the company's corporate clients. When he received last-minute tickets that no one could use, he offered them to his staff.

From Dave Powers
To MarComm Mail Group
Subject Today's Quiz

One of the media vendors was in this morning and gave me 4 tickets for the Harlem Globetrotters this Saturday at 1:30 at the Civic Center. Since Sales can't use them, I will give away two blocks of two to a couple of you. Please select the correct answer for the following question from the list below. We will take the third caller and any other correct answers to distribute the tickets. As a tiebreaker, state in one sentence why you want to go. All entries must be postmarked one month from today.

Question: The Harlem Globetrotters play what sport?

A) Race Walking
B) Horse Racing
C) Horsing Around
D) World Travel
E) Basketball

From	Lee Chang
To	Dave Powers
Cc	MarComm Mail Group
Subject	Re: Today's Quiz

If you have any tickets left, I could use two. In China, where I was born, we played hockey all the time.

From	Dave Powers
To	Lee Chang
Cc	MarComm Mail Group
Subject	Re: Today's Quiz

Lee, it sounds like you've been away from the mother country oolong.

Chapter 13

Taking the Plunge

At their customary Friday night dinner date, Dave told Elisa about Al's push for him to take a full-time position with the company. He explained the details that Al offered him, but he was still torn.

Elisa had been thinking about this consulting contract and her running the agency pretty much on her own. She said, "David, I know how you feel about owning the business, and maintaining your independence, but there's more to the picture. A generous benefits package is very important to us right now, and you would be making a good salary now plus a better one in two years. Also, the cost of living is certainly lower in Rhode Island than in New Jersey. Even if I only held onto a few accounts, we could keep some semblance of the agency and be in a comfortable position. You're loving what you're doing there. I think you should go for it."

Her comments pushed him over the top. "I agree. Let's do it. We'll sell the agency, move to Rhode Island, and see if we can pick up a few small accounts up there that you can run."

"That makes the most sense. However, I think we should rent our house here for a year or two in case the job doesn't work out. And then sell it."

"Good idea. Now, let me tell you about another opportunity I uncovered in Providence. I had a meeting with a guy who started a website called findRI.com. He wants RIHIP to advertise on it. And at my suggestion he's going to run a humor column that I will create. It will give me some exposure that you can utilize to capture some small clients up here."

Chapter 14

The Bag Kick-Off

With Wendy's glowing endorsement of the pharmacy bag program, Dave called in his production manager, Denise and explained the details of the program. He suggested that the bag graphics include only the RIHIP Medicare logo. Handing her Steve Fisher's card, he told her to call him and move ahead with the project.

A few hours later, Jack Landrieu called Dave to thank him for the business, and said he would accompany Steve to this first meeting with the production people. He wanted to be sure the program began smoothly, became successful, and ran indefinitely.

The next morning, Jack and Steve met with Denise and her assistant Gail, went over the details, and put the project in motion. The two men then stopped by Dave's office to say hello and again thank Dave for the order. During this brief meeting, Jack confirmed that the $50,000 order for one million bags would last about six months. Quickly doing the math in his head, Dave realized that at $50 per 1,000 impressions, this was really low-cost advertising. A promotion like this should cost three of four times as much. It was targeted to an important audience, plus the program will be delivering a benefit to an adversarial group of providers. *Win, win.*

Following the meeting, Dave sent Wendy a confirming email and gave her the exact pricing and initial timeframe. Her response was again very positive, and she expressed the hope that the program worked well and would continue for some time into the future.

Within a week, Steve sent over proofs of the bag with the logo in position. Dave had Denise send some of the samples over to Wendy to show her staff.

Chapter 15

Mass Communications

At the weekly Marketing Communications staff meeting, Dave announced the new pharmacy bag program and passed around the samples. Everyone thought it was a brilliant concept. The department was on a roll.

All the new staff members were enthusiastic about the opportunity to express their creativity and they offered wonderful ideas for other campaigns. The philosophy that Dave introduced when he first arrived at RIHIP was that everyone has creative ideas, and he encouraged the team members to speak out at their meetings and offer up any concepts that they considered viable.

As a result of this freedom, the department had developed some truly innovative recommendations, some of which emerged into programs that were, until now, unimagined in the health insurance industry. And some of them came from the clerical and production staff, and not just the writers and designers.

The urge to educate the company's subscribers on how enhanced lifestyles and habits results in better health, a brilliant concept emerged at one of the staff meetings. Marketing Communications introduced a quarterly magazine that was supported by advertising. It started with an original press run of 200,000 copies to be distributed to every subscriber family in the state.

Hospitals, clinics, physician groups, and other health-related organizations immediately, began to place advertising in the magazine. Then Dave got a call from the VP of Marketing at CVS Pharmacy. He wanted to permanently book the back cover position. He also wanted the press run increased by 50,000, so they could put free copies in all Rhode Island's CVS pharmacies for increased distribution.

The enthusiastic response to the magazine from both within and outside the company triggered another breakout idea. A sister program in the form of a series of TV specials began to take shape. When Dave presented this ambitious concept to Joan Rotino, she was ecstatic. She brought him right into the CEO's office to tell him about the idea.

A smiling Al Conover came around his desk and warmly shook Dave's hand, saying, "Dave, no employee has ever impacted this company as fast as you have with such creativity. I'm confident we'll generate enough profit this year to give you the promotion I promised."

Joan sat and glowed, while Dave absorbed Al's gratitude and appreciation.

Leaving the office that day, Dave was overwhelmed with his accomplishments and Al's appreciation of his efforts.

Al's comments made all the angst I get dealing with these slackers worthwhile. While I love being an entrepreneur, this job gives me creative freedom and I couldn't be happier. This unrestricted autonomy is enabling me to achieve the height of my career!

Chapter16

That Secret Spring in Maine

When Dave came back from a lunch meeting at the ad agency, he checked his email and saw a note from Cindy Sward, one of his senior writers on the department email account.

From	Cindy Sward
Date	10/04/97 11:21 AM
To	MarComm Mail Group
Subject	Free Water Cooler

I just came from the Business Expo where I got an offer we can't refuse. At the Poland Springs booth, the rep, upon learning I work for RIHIP, offered us free water and a cooler at no cost for a month. If we decide to continue the service, we just have to pay for the water we use, and they will not charge us to rent the cooler. If ten or more people are interested, I'll order the service.

Dave laughed and responded.

From	Dave Powers
Date	10/04/97 02:05 PM

To	Cindy Sward
cc	MarComm Mail Group
Subject	Re: Free Water Cooler

Free water cooler? Did he offer you free air also? The company doesn't charge anyone rentals for the cooler. They make their money from the water, which they get *free* from their spring in that secret location in Maine. Of course, all the moose in Maine know the secret location. They use it as a toilet every day. That being said, the water is still better than the sludge that comes out of the spigots in our building.

I don't drink much water. Elisa says it's good for your complexion, reduces blood pressure, and helps weight loss. If I thought it would grow hair, I'd probably bathe in it, but count me in. I'm good for one or two ounces a day.

From	Eric Wilson
To	Cindy Sward
Cc	MarComm Mail Group
Subject	Re: Free Water Cooler

I know I should be looking forward to drinking "designer" water – it might help me create better brochure layouts. But I like the tap water here. It's how I get my recommended daily allotment of vitamins and minerals.

From	Lee Chang
To	Cindy Sward
Cc	MarComm Mail Group
Subject	Re: Free Water Cooler

If Eric is going to design better because he drinks this water, then I should too. Eric, how many glasses will it take to be as good as you?

Old School Perspective

Dick Nichols was walking to his office as Joan passed by. He looked up and said, "Do you have a minute? I want to talk to you about these custom coverage packages we're offer to our corporate clients."

Instead of sitting at the conference table in his office, he went to his chair behind his desk and pointed to one of the visitor chairs opposite him. The snub did not go unnoticed.

Without any preamble, Dick went right into his concern. "I'm seeing a growing number of contracts coming through that deviate from our standard coverage contract. Why is that?"

"Yes, that's true. My sales team and the brokers are working diligently to recover all the accounts we've lost over the last few years. And we're willing to do whatever it takes to get them back."

"That's bullshit! It takes hours of time to write the code for all these changes, and that costs us a fortune. I want you to stop this choice, and only offer the standard policies."

"You know Dick, that's the kind of thinking that got us in trouble in the first place. You have a team of code writers sitting on their butts and not doing any work. I happen to know that it doesn't take that much time to edit the terms of a policy. My nephew runs a computer department for the V.A. in Washington and they're making changes all the time without much effort."

Dick waved her off, saying, "That's different."

"It is like hell. We're getting enormous responses from former clients because we're willing to modify our insurance coverage to meet their unique needs. It shows them that we want the business and will do what's necessary to earn it. My division is pulling this company out of bankruptcy, and you're bitching about spending a few bucks on coding."

Standing, she continued, "Why don't you go play golf and leave the real management to us." And with that she stormed out leaving Dick speechless.

Chapter 18

Dream House Rental

Elisa sounded very excited when she phoned Dave. "I just got a call from a guy in New York City. He's the CEO of a technology company and he wants to rent our house with an option to buy it."

"That's incredible. It sounds like a perfect offer."

"Yes, they are coming out Saturday morning to see the house and discuss terms."

"Okay. Why don't you call a cleaning service to do the floors and windows. And let's talk about it at our Friday night dinner date."

Eating Peking Duck at LookSee Restaurant, Elisa shared what she knew of the rental prospect. They were a young couple with a five-year-old son and a three-year-old daughter. The wife was pregnant, and the husband wanted a house with enough property to build a play area with swings and slides and maybe a tree house for the kids. They would like to sign a two-year lease with the option to buy any time after the first year.

The family showed up at eleven on Saturday morning and immediately fell in love with the house and wooded setting. They even wanted to keep the furniture and pay for it as part of the purchase agreement. They shook hands and Dave said, I will have a lease-purchase agreement drawn up and sent to you. And you can move in within 30 days.

After they left, Elisa hugged Dave. "This is an ideal scenario for us. I'll get busy and see if we can sell the agency right away."

Chapter 19

Debut Column

When Dave posted his first column on findRI.com, the website got dozens of comments as the report captured the quirks of the residents of the state. With that response, he decided to share it with his staff.

> **From**   Dave Powers
> **To**   MarComm Mail Group
> **Cc**
> **Subject** *Local Color* Column

Who Moved My Salami?

I read this must-read book a while back. It was called *Who Moved My Cheese?* It was about this mouse that got his whiskers bunched up because someone moved his cheese to another spot. When the mouse couldn't find his cheese in the usual place, he became confused, paranoid and angry. As I read the book, I concluded that this mouse was dumber than dirt. When I finished reading it, I yawned and threw the book in the trash, feeling that I was a victim of all the hype about this breakthrough approach to dealing with change.

Being a food lover, the book gave me pause when I thought about what if something like this happened to people. Say you went into a supermarket and the robbies were now in the pet food section. (If you're unfamiliar with *robbies*, it is broccoli rabe, a somewhat bitter cousin to broccoli.) I had never heard it called robbies before moving to Rhode Island. I guess it's part of the local vernacular. It's in the same category as *cabinets* and *stuffies*, two other words that I would never have expected to find on a restaurant menu.

Where would you be if they moved all the Dunkin' Donuts shops? You drive *downcity* to your favorite shop and find it's been moved to the top floor of a six-story walk-up. And what's with all the donut shops anyway? With Dunkin' Donuts, Honey Dew, Bess Eaton, Allie's and now Krispy Kremes, we have more donut shops per capita than any other state in the country.

Next time you go to Federal Hill and pick up a dry salami off the counter in Venda Ravioli, think about how easy it was, and how you didn't have to get all stressed out finding a dry cleaner that sold it.

There, now you don't have to read the book.

Chapter 20

IBM Golf Gig

Dave got a call from Charles Latham, VP Human Resources inviting him to a golf event. "Dave, the account rep from IBM called Dick Nichols with an opportunity to play at The International in Bolton, Massachusetts. Dick just asked me to play and suggested I invite you and Billy as well. It will include dinner afterwards."

Dave had been playing golf with Charlie, Dick and CIO Billy Boffone about once or twice a month at either Charlie's club or Dick's. Nichols and Latham were both single-digit handicap golfers, while Billy and Dave scored in the teens. With Dick, the game came easy as he played golf three or four times a week. Charlie, who only got out on weekends, had to work harder at his game. His after-hours practice, on his residence course, however, paid off for him. The four men always enjoyed the camaraderie of their Saturday mornings together. He looked forward to playing at this legendary club.

The golf event was made up of twelve foursomes from different IBM clients and included a competition and prizes. The RIHIP team took first place, with each member winning a new golf bag emblazoned with the IBM logo. The cocktails and dinner festivities were a raucous affair, and the Rhode Islanders were among the last to leave.

Sitting at the bar afterwards, Dick turned to Dave "It's a great way to earn a living, isn't it? Here we are getting paid to play golf and enhance our relationship with one of our largest vendors."

Dave responded, "This was certainly fun and a great break from the office. But I think working at RIHIP, for me anyway, is a terrific way to earn a living. It's non-stop fun."

"Powers, there must be something wrong with you. Work is a tedious pain. And what kind of accent is that? It's certainly different from any of the Rhode Island dialects."

"It's my upbringing. Elisa and I are both immigrants. She was born in Italy, and I was born in Brooklyn." And as they broke out laughing with that revelation, he added, "Let me buy the nightcap and toast all the accents from Boston to Brooklyn."

Chapter 21

Glowing Report

The National Health Insurance Association sent out an announcement letter on the first of May. It was addressed to Al Conover, with a copy sent to Dave Powers. The letter congratulated RIHIP on its first-place finish for its advertising campaign, *Your Health. For Life.* Dave immediately called Bruce Dane, the CEO at the ad agency and told him about the award. He then brought the letter into that morning's staff meeting and shared the news with his crew.

"Marketing Communications is on a roll! And I couldn't be more delighted with this team of talented professionals. We've had a great string of successes and it is making a huge difference in the company's sales efforts. So, let's toast our creativity and build upon these triumphs.

I also want to share another department milestone with all of you. Kathy Cormier, who runs all the company meetings, just got her Event Planning Certification. And although I didn't get a certificate you've probably already concluded that I am also certified."

The next day Dave attended the Senior Staff meeting, which was held in the company's huge boardroom. The conference table could easily seat 30 attendees, plus room for dozens more people along the walls. He noticed the usual pattern of attendance. He made it a practice to arrive early to this and every meeting. Phil Lyons, as expected, was absent. Al Conover and Joan always arrived just before the starting time. And Dick Nichols made a habit of coming in late.

At the meeting, Al read the letter from the Association, and delivered a glowing assessment of Dave's role in RIHIP's turnaround. The group broke out into applause, which Dave had not expected. Dave acknowledged the accolade and responded, "The success we're experiencing is a team effort. I have a terrific group of communications specialists, and Joan has been building an excellent sales department that is receiving the support of the other divisions. This company-wide synergy is how we get these superior results."

Dave looked around and spotted Dick looking away with a morbid expression.

Al then asked Dave to give a report on all the activities his department had been undertaking. Not being expected to report at today's meeting, Dave did not have a full report ready. But he intimately knew every program that was in effect. He quickly ran through the TV advertising campaign, the prescription bag promotion, the new quarterly magazine program, and the upcoming one-hour TV specials. He also explained the new product literature initiative and all the other smaller programs.

The CFO stared blankly and nervously twisted his watch.

"Don't worry," Dave said, "When I arrived here, RIHIP was losing market share daily, and my recommendation was to launch an intensive campaign to get people's attention. It was the only way we were going to break through the clutter and turn sales around after so many years of neglect. And now we are not only substantially growing our book of business, but also setting national records with the new Medicare insurance products. And I'm still way under my budget."

Chapter 22

Troubling Announcement

The next week, Joan sounded distressed when she called Dave into her office. For years, he had collaborated with her on various projects at different companies where she worked. Joan was pure sales. She abhorred detail, but if she decided to sell you something, you were going to buy it.

Joan wasn't selling anything today. "This morning Al Conover called me and the other two EVPs into his office and abruptly announced his retirement."

Dave was shocked. "What? Why?"

"He said the decision was driven by his wife's declining health." Joan went on to explain his sudden announcement had left them speechless and wondering who would be named to replace him.

After thinking about it, Dave, took it in stride. Although Al had been his champion during his early days adjusting to the culture, he felt he could now function on his own. His successes and the changes he engineered with the purchasing department made Dave feel confident that he could navigate the corporate landmines. He was settling into the culture and lifestyle of Rhode Island.

Now that Elisa lived with him in a furnished apartment in East Greenwich, he was thinking about buying a house. They had sold the agency, albeit for less money than they expected, and they were ready to establish roots in Rhode Island. Despite the slight trepidation caused by Al's announcement, Dave felt confident they were on the right path.

But on that morning, he had no idea how his world was about to change.

Chapter 23
You've Got Mail

Dave was in the graphic design department when his assistant came in to tell him that House Speaker Landrieu was on the phone. Dave went into his office to take the call. "Well hello Jack. How are you?"

"I'm doing great, thanks. But I have some good news for you. Can we meet for lunch today? I want to share a letter with you."

"Sure. I'm open for lunch. Where do you want to meet?"

"How about The Capital Grill at noon? See you then."

Dave grinned, knowing that The Capital Grill, which was down the hill from the state house, was one of the most expensive restaurants in Providence, and the power restaurant for all Rhode Island's politicians.

Arriving a few minutes after twelve, the maître d' brought Dave right to Jack's table. Although he noticed that Landrieu was having a cocktail, he opted for an iced tea. Back in the *Mad Men* days in New York City, Dave drank heavily, along with all his business acquaintances. But ultimately, he realized that the lack of functionality in the afternoons and at night was not worth the pleasure of the drinks. So now wine was his drink of choice and only in the evening. He often shared this theory he had. "Everyone had a certain quantity of alcohol that they could consume in their lifetime, and I'm convinced that I had reached his quota by age thirty-five."

After both men ordered, Jack pulled a letter from his briefcase and handed it to Dave with a big smile. The letter was from a pharmacy owner in Woonsocket. It was in response to receiving his first order of prescription bags from RIHIP. He expressed his gratitude to the company for sponsoring and funding the program. He was delighted that RIHIP took this extraordinary step to support the local pharmacies in Rhode Island. And as a member of the Board of the Independent Pharmacy Owners, he was going to push the board towards better cooperation with RIHIP.

When they completed lunch, Jack reiterated his invitation to take Dave out for a round of golf. Dave concurred saying, "Yes, but before I accept your invitation to play, I must ask, are there houses along your golf course?" Seeing the puzzled look on Landrieu's face, he explained with a smirk, "I been using use those new Microsoft golf balls. They're attracted to windows."

From the restaurant, Dave went straight to Wendy's office to show her the letter. She read it, and looked at him with a smile, "You have come up with so many innovative programs, and the results are just awesome. I can't tell you how much this reaction from a local pharmacist means to me. Keep up the outstanding work."

Chapter 24

Top-Flight Bushes

From	Dave Powers
Date	11/17/97 07:01 AM
To	MarComm Mail Group
Subject	RIHIP Golf Tournament

Saturday was the Annual RIHIP Golf Tournament. Representing Marketing Communications, the crack team of Eric Wilson and Dave Powers set out to tear up the course and win the tournament. Unfortunately, it didn't work out as planned.

At Eric's suggestion, the seemingly invincible team started out drinking beer at 7:30 when they arrived at the course. Dave was never a guy who could handle an abundance of alcohol, especially in the morning.

He may tell you a different story, but his terrible play caused the breakdown. During the round they lost nineteen balls playing eighteen holes. And Dave claimed that Eric lost most of them. But in his defense, when they both ran out of balls, it was Eric who scoured the bushes along the fairways. He explained that in Rhode Island, they plant special bushes that grow Top-Flight balls. He found enough of these budget priced balls for them to complete the round. It made Dave wonder why they didn't plant Titleist bushes. Those golf balls are much more expensive.

At the conclusion of the tournament, the MarComm Twosome finished in thirty-fourth place out of thirty-six teams. Even the women's teams beat them.

Chapter 25

Smoke Out

Dave sat in a meeting Wendy Ketler scheduled to discuss a smoking cessation issue with teenagers. Members of her wellness team shared statistics about the increase in smoking among this group. While most categories were reducing their smoking, teenagers were getting into this deadly habit in alarming numbers. After presenting their report, the chairperson turned to Dave. "We need you to come up with a communications program to convince teenagers that it is not cool to smoke, and it could have fatal consequences later in life."

Before he spoke, Dave looked around the room making eye contact with everyone in attendance. "Teenagers think they are bulletproof and that they'll live forever. This group doesn't accept advice from adults, and they certainly aren't going to respond to anything we say."

Nodding, Wendy said, "Yes. You've just articulated our challenge. Now, how are we going to get through to them?"

"Let me discuss it to my team. They are very creative thinkers. We'll come up with something and get back to you."

Dave presented the issue at their next weekly meeting, and everyone became animated. Most of them had smoked as teenagers, and a few still smoked. After listening to each other's descriptions of what wouldn't work, Charlene, the department's clerical assistant reluctantly offered her idea. "We need a superhero. It's the only way we'll get their attention."

Everyone's positive reaction caused her to light up with a huge smile. It was her first contribution to the creative process, and it triggered an outpouring of ideas from around the table based on her concept.

With no clear winner among the suggestions, Dave ended the meeting with his directive. "I want you all to be thinking of ways to implement Charlene's concept. Everything you've come up with involves contracting with a rock star. This project will be a five-figure promotion, not a seven-figure extravaganza. Let that guide you."

After the meeting Dave called Alan Randolph from findRI.com and told him about the smoking cessation program. "I'm looking for an undiscovered rock star that will appeal to teenagers and make them consider not smoking or to stop smoking. Somebody that's on the cusp of greatness and is still affordable."

"That's a terrific undertaking. I want to be involved with my website. And I have an idea. I'll call you tomorrow."

Chapter 26

Getting the Boot

Dave was sitting at the bar when Alan Randolph walked in with his surprise guest. As Dave slid off the barstool, Alan approached and said, "Dave Powers meet Adam Vinatieri."

Sharing a strong handshake, they looked at each other, nodded, and smiled. Dave said, "Let's move to a table."

Once seated, they ordered drinks and Alan opened the conversation. "Dave, I told Adam about the smoking cessation program and your need for a celebrity spokesperson. He's very interested."

Adam added, "Yes, I'd like to know more but I like the idea of working with young people. Of course, I have major commitments during football season, so my time may be limited."

As Adam spoke, Dave is looking at this handsome man, not much older than the teenagers the company is trying to reach. At about Dave's height, Adam carried a solid-built, muscular frame. He had dark hair and a mischievous smile. Dave said, "I'm planning on a one-year program of appearances, public service TV commercials, and a few live events. And yes, we can work around your schedule."

"That sound great. It's about what I was expecting. Football season is about to start, so is there any way we can launch this program in January or February?"

"While I was hoping to launch this fall, I knew that would be almost impossible."

The two men continued to discuss details of the proposed campaign, and Alan added a few recommendations including the suggestion that Adam could possibly shoot the TV ads during the team's bye week in December. Dave responded positively to that.

Once he was comfortable with his role in the program, Adam offered to participate for one year at a $50,000 fee. Dave responded, "Adam, that is very generous of you. It will really help this noble cause."

I'm excited about this project. I haven't done anything like it before, and I'm looking forward to working with these kids."

After meeting Adam, Dave began to follow the Patriots. The team was playing well and, in the hunt to make the playoffs. Watching one of the night games during the playoffs, Dave said to Elisa, "A few weeks ago, we produced some TV commercials with Adam Vinatieri. He was a little nervous starting out, but once he relaxed, he came across very sincere."

"What did you expect? Not everyone is a frustrated actor who can't wait to get in front of a camera, like you."

Watching the final games of the season, Dave became very excited. Adam scored the tying field goal and the winning field goal to put the Patriots into the Super Bowl. And his kick at the end of the game made the Patriots the Super Bowl Champs!

Dave turned to Elisa and said, "Adam Vinatieri is the hero of the season and the Super Bowl, and the TV campaign starring Adam starts tomorrow. Everyone at RIHIP will think I'm a genius."

Chapter 27

Selling the Board

The unscheduled board meeting was called within a week of Al's announcement for the purpose of selecting an executive search committee to recruit a new CEO. None of the Senior Staff members who usually made reports at board meetings were invited. However, Dick Nichols as EVP and the protégé of Al Conover requested an opportunity to address the board.

A handful of the executives, including Dave met at a small neighborhood bar across the street from RIHIP headquarters and awaited Dick to meet up with them and report on his discussion with the board. Dave was the lowest ranking attendee at the large table where they sat, had drinks, and snacked on appetizers. His growing friendship with Nichols piqued his interest in the outcome of his appearance at the meeting.

About an hour later, Dick came into the bar with a big grin. He ordered a bourbon on the rocks and shared his interaction with the board.

"When I told the board I had an important message for them, they agreed to listen to my pitch. First, I reminded them that the company was in a precarious position, being in the early stages of a recovery after three years of $25 million losses. And we would lose that momentum while awaiting the selection of a new CEO, plus additional time for him to get up to speed. I had been groomed for the CEO position by Al and was fully prepared to take the reins and continue on our current path to success. I also agreed to accept the position on an interim basis for six months if I don't meet expectations. Al confirmed my statements and strongly endorsed me. The chairman then asked me to wait in my office while they discussed my offer and decide next steps."

Dick reached for his drink and took a sip as Billy Boffone commented, "You must have been sweating just sitting around waiting to be called back in."

"Oh, yeah. It was nearly an hour before they brought me back in. The chairman agreed with my assessment of the situation, as they were very concerned about interrupting the recent success, we've achieved plus putting the company in limbo for months until they could find a suitable candidate. They recognized the advantage of my working knowledge of the company, and they accepted my offer."

Everyone cheered and then Dick then added, "They offered me the interim position with one caveat. My wife, who is an AVP in Facilities Division, can no longer work for the company. I told them that it would not be a problem. She would be terminated promptly."

As he made the comments about his wife, Dave sensed a quiver from Joan, but when he looked at her, she still wore her broad, engaging smile. Everyone around the table, stood and queued up to shake Dick's hand. When it was Dave's turn, he said, "Congratulations, Dick. I will support you with all the energy I gave to Al's administration. And I'm hoping your new role will still allow some time for golf. I've been enjoying playing with you."

"Thanks, Dave. And don't worry about the golf. Nothing will ever change there."

When they were all seated again, Charlie Latham lifted his glass and said, "Here's to Dick. We all support you! After that, the party began to break up. As they were leaving, Joan quietly asked Dave to meet her for coffee in her office at eight the next morning. Knowing that Joan never got to the office before 9:30, Dave knew it must be important.

Driving home Dave thought about this turn of events. *I was a little apprehensive when Al resigned, thinking about some bureaucrat stranger coming in and changing everything. But now I feel good with Dick taking over. He even mentioned that the golf will continue. Elisa will also be relieved.*

Chapter 28

All About Dick

Arriving at Joan's office before the activity in the C-Suite really began functioning, Dave was anxious to hear what Joan wanted to share with him. Before coming into her office, he made a cup of tea in the executive kitchenette, where Joan, despite the presence of the 30-cup urn of fresh-brewed coffee, had made her usual mug of instant Taster's Choice a few minutes earlier. *Ugh!*

Sitting at her conference table, Dave commented, "Wasn't that an interesting evening? We all expected the board would punt and establish a long vetting process for a new CEO. And that would have stifled the sales momentum the company had generated over the past year. How did Dick pull it off?"

"Well, here's what you need to know about Dick. First of all, I'm certain that Al gave him a couple of months heads-up on his resignation. This gave Dick a chance to cozy up to the key members of the board. He probably took some of the men out for a round of golf and drinks. And he certainly invited each of the few women who sit on the board to a private dinner. And you can bet he used his charisma to flirt with them, despite the 20-odd year age differences.

"Dick can be very charming, and he uses that appeal and his good looks to his best advantage. He talks sports and politics with the guys. And he convinces the women that under different circumstances, he'd be inviting them to his bedroom. So, he obviously went into the boardroom with well more than half the members already on his side. And was prepared to sell the others. He played them like he plays his concert piano."

"That's the second time you mentioned Dick's piano playing. Is he that good?"

"Oh, yes. He played for us at the Christmas party at his home last year. And he was every bit as good at the piano as he is at golf. He practices every night."

"That is interesting. You're filling my head with stuff I didn't know about Dick. And I've become one of his golf buddies. I didn't read him like that at all. I've watched him in Senior Staff meetings, and he always seems disinterested, except when there's an issue regarding his area of control, Operations. On the golf course, he never talks about work. It's always golf and any of the current sports news."

"Let me take you deeper into Dick's persona, "Despite being with the company for over 20 years, Dick still doesn't get the nuances of the current state of health insurance. He's old school and thinks because we were the first insurer in the state, everyone wants our coverage. He doesn't appreciate how strong the competition has become, despite them having taken away forty percent of our subscriber base in a few short years. He discourages us from negotiating contracts, offer incentives, or customize policies for our larger groups. He feels that causes extra work for the IT department. They have to write code for special benefits, billing changes, etc. And he sees that effort as a waste of money."

"What? That's small-minded thinking. What could that cost?"

"Exactly. To understand Dick, you should know more about his background. Al met him when he was a high school dropout, caddying at Al's country club. He took a liking to him and hired him on the condition that he would get his GED, and then go for a college degree. Dick took the offer and quickly got the equivalency diploma. But he stalled on enrolling in college. After pressure from Al, he finally signed up at Rhode Island Community College and got a two-year associate degree which he barely passed, I heard."

"Well, that doesn't make him a bad guy. I don't have a degree. My early business failures were my college education. And let me tell you, it was expensive tuition."

Laughing, Joan continued, "Al started Dick out in Operations, which has always been our largest division. And every time someone retired, he promoted Dick up the ladder. This of course, caused resentment as others felt they deserved the promotions over him. But Dick survived with his winning personality. And now he's the CEO, but he really doesn't have the requisite knowledge. That said we're better with a known quantity, rather than bringing in an outsider that would want to disrupt everything. And besides, I'm confident that I can control him. I know how to play to his flirtatious ways."

"Okay, so how is he going to change the status quo? And what should we do to influence his decision-making?"

"Good Thinking! Dick is going to be very focused on his own success. So, he won't interfere with our sales strategy. I've already discussed this with him. If we continue to increase sales, we'll be very profitable and that will reflect well for him. He knows nothing about marketing, so you will be able to move forward with your creative programs unabated. He also has no contact with the ad agency, doesn't really know Bruce Dane very well. In that way, your relationship there will remain intact. And keep playing golf with Dick, every chance you get. Invite him to some of the charitable outings you play in."

"That's easy."

"Dave, his appointment is going to work out just great for you. I just know it."

Afterwards, Dave thought about his conversation with her. *All she ever sees are moonbeams and fairy dust through those rose-colored glasses. I sure hope she's right.*

Chapter 29

Planting the Rumor

Later that same morning, Phil Lyons sat in Dick Nichols office to discuss an important issue. Phil explained that he was getting intel from a trusted source in the legislature that there were discussions taking place regarding RIHIP. A group of influential politicians wanted the state to take over the insurer and run it as a single-payer system. With the company's recent losses, the timing seemed opportune. And this group was salivating over control they would have over the vast sums of money that health care transacted.

Dick became alarmed. This was a serious threat to the company's independence. "We have got to take immediate action. Call in the outside lobbyists and other consultants to tackle this problem. And move fast!"

Phil agreed and also suggest that they substantially increase the amount of money in their PAC so there would be a war chest to fund all necessary cash distributions. Dick immediately approved the idea and told Phil to have one of his team members make a presentation at the next Senior Staff meeting.

Phil suggested, "We need to have each of them write a check for $1,000 and also hand in $1,000 in cash. Then the company will work out a reimbursement for the executives with a bonus program." He also asked Dick to double the company budget for the PAC. They concluded the meeting with a discussion about expanding Phil's department.

In a rare show of emotion, Lyons returned to his office, closed the door and fist-pumped the air.

It worked to perfection. All Jack Landrieu's coaching since I got here is working exactly as we planned. Now I finally feel secure in my job.

Chapter 30

Free Lunch

A memo went around the company advising the staff that on the coming Friday, before the Christmas holiday, the cafeteria was providing is annual Christmas lunch for all employees. When Dave read the memo, he thought his team would rather celebrate with each other in their conference room rather than go to the cafeteria. With unanimous approval of his idea, he assured the staff the cost would be the same as the company luncheon.

From   Dave Powers
To   MarComm Mail Group
Subject Luncheon Accounting

Dear Overstuffed Elves,
After Lucy went overboard and ordered too much expensive food, we did the fuzzy math and I realized that she charged over $10,000 on my credit card. No, really. Do you have any idea what braised armadillo ribs cost? Or koala bear salad?

Anyway, I decided to make the luncheon my treat. It's my way of saying *Thank You* for doing such a terrific job and making our department the professional, award-winning organization that it has become.

Of course, Donna had a lot to do with it. She patiently waded through all the wannabes, has-beens, and pretenders and hired the best talent around.

Happy Holidays to all. Ho, ho, ho!

From Donna Marino
To Dave Powers
Subject Re: Luncheon Accounting

Well, Mr. Sandy Claws, you didn't fool me. When I saw all that exotic food you were ordering, I knew there was no way it would cost the same as the company luncheon. You had to have something else up your sleeve besides your knobby elbow.

Thank you for your thoughtfulness and your kind words. I'm delighted to be here and to be part of this exciting team.

Chapter 31

Hired Gun

Recognizing that he had no close confidants in the highest levels of management at the company, Dick took some drastic steps to remedy the situation. He hired the lead attorney of RIHIP's outside law firm, Andrew Westbrook, and named him Chief Operating Officer. He and Andy had become good friends over the years, both from their business dealings and their frequent golf outings.

In his meetings with Andy leading up to the appointment, Dick explained the Senior Staff structure and his disdain for most of the executives. Other than the VPs from his division, his parochial thinking convinced him the other VPs and EVPs were ineffective and self-focused.

For his part, Andy had extensive knowledge of the legal aspects of the health insurance process, but no knowledge of the business functions within the firm. And he had no practical administrative or management experience.

When he mentioned his decision to the EVPs, they wondered how this newly hired number-two person on the org chart was going to contribute to the company's success. They also felt slighted that they were not chosen, and they were miffed that there was now another layer of management inserted above them with no perceived benefit.

Chapter 32

The New Lyons Den

Dave awakened his computer upon his arrival at the office on what promised to be a quiet Wednesday following the Christmas holiday. The first communication he read was an all-employee memo from Dick Nichols. It was his first as the new CEO.

The email announced the promotion of Phil Lyons to Executive Vice President of the Legislative Affairs Division. The significance of referring to one of the smallest *departments* in the company as a *division* was not lost on Dave. It consisted of Lyons, his two assistants, who did most of the lobbying at the state house, and their secretary. By comparison, the Provider Relations Division had nearly 600 people, the Operations Division included more than 1,100 staff, and the Sales & Marketing Division had well over 300.

The memo did go on to explain that as CEO, Dick saw the need to increase the importance, size, and budget of Legislative Affairs. He recognized a possible threat to the company's ability to make unencumbered decisions from legislation that could be harmful to the firm's interests. His goal therefore was to add an educational component to the lobbying, so the senators and representatives would be able to make more informed decisions on health care matters.

After studying the memo, Dave concluded that Lyons' *division* was going to need the expertise and services of his communications department. Looks like he was getting a new internal client. He immediately drafted a congratulatory note to Phil Lyons on his promotion.

Chapter 33

Shuffling the Deck Chairs

Dave found another all-employee email in his file that morning from Dick which shocked him.

From   Richard F. Nichols
To   All Employees
Subject Restructure

In a crucial effort to improve corporate efficiency and accommodate the wishes of several Senior Staff members, I am restructuring and reducing the size of Senior Staff. Most of the departing executives are exercising an early retirement option, and the others are leaving for opportunities outside the company. We will shrink the Executive Committee from thirty-three vice presidents to sixteen, as well as eliminating some of the other executive positions. The remaining VPs will be given additional responsibility as we consolidate management tasks.

As part of the restructure, I am announcing the addition of a new executive that has joined the company to add strength and support to areas of weakness within our ranks. Andy Westbrook, from Prendergast & Marden, PA, has accepted the position of Chief Operating Officer. Andy, who many of you know, has been our outside legal consultant for several years.

Also, I have promoted Philip Lyons to Senior Vice President of Government Relations.

Under the new structure, all vice presidents will report to Andy Westbrook, except Phil Lyons. Due to the critical nature of our legislative affairs, Phil will report directly to me.

This restructuring of responsibilities will take place over the next two months and each department will be notified as specific changes are implemented. Organizational charts are being distributed that will show the new chain of command in each division.

Richard F. Nichols
President & CEO

Dave read the memo and became very angry thinking about it. *I can't believe he chose to tear Senior Staff apart during the holidays and without notice. How could he be such a heartless bastard!*

Chapter 34

The Exchange Rate

As everyone was getting ready to leave the office that day for the New Year's weekend, another memo appeared in Dave's inbox. This one, also from Dick was addressed to all Senior Staff members. The note announced that Marci Nichols had resigned from her position as Facilities AVP and was leaving the company effective immediately. Dick cited the requirement put down by the board, that the company could no longer employ Marci, since she was his wife. Dave was shocked at the speed with which Dick moved to follow this directive to terminate his spouse. He also noted that the memo went out at the end of the day, long after most of the staff had left for the long weekend.

The note went on to mention that in moving to the CEO's office, he was appointing a new secretary for himself. His former assistant would remain in the executive secretary pool and continue to serve the other VPs in the C-Suite.

Dick had selected Louise Vargas to be his secretary. She was very attractive with dark hair, sparkling brown eyes and a warm smile. Her looks were strikingly similar to Dick's wife, possibly because they were both of Portuguese extraction. Even their body shapes were nearly the same. In fact, early on he once confused them at a gathering until Louise spoke to him. He quickly realized that she did not have the polished communication skills that Marci had.

Before Dave finished reading the memo, his phone rang with Joan on the line. She asked if he could come to her office before leaving for the New Year's weekend.

When he arrived at the executive offices, everyone was already gone, including all the support staff. Walking into Joan's office, he could see that she was upset. Through gritted teeth she spat out, "Did you read Dick's new memo? How could he do this to her?"

Not knowing what was going on, he sat there not comprehending the situation. Joan filled him in.

"As much as I like Dick, his major shortcoming has always been his infidelity. And I have no tolerance for that. His marriage to Marci has always been rocky, as she has caught him fooling around a number of times. About ten years ago, he moved out, leaving her for some brainless twit with big boobs. And at the time, he told Marci that he was going to divorce her. The company was much smaller then, so everyone knew what was going on."

"Jeez, how could he live with himself?

" I know. Can you believe it? Al Conover stepped in and called Dick into his office, closed the door and told him, 'If you ever want to be president of RIHIP, you get back to your wife and make this marriage work.' Dick chose his career over a pair of melons and dumped the girlfriend. The appearance of the marriage improved but not the substance. Dick continued to have his flings, and Marci chose to ignore them."

"I've heard rumors about some of that."

"Now let me fast-forward. The directive from the board is bogus. Dick had one of his golf buddies on the board ask about the nepotism conflict with a spouse reporting to an executive. Technically, this is not an issue, as she wouldn't be reporting directly to him, anyway. But Dick told the board he would resolve it to avoid any optics issue. I know this because I have more friends on the board than he has. I also know that he is going to divorce Marci immediately. And his new flame is? Yep, it's Louise, and they will move in together as soon as the decree is final."

"Holy Shit! I always see women flirting with him around the office, but knowing his wife, I could never see him stepping out of line. She's beautiful, smart and charming."

"Dave, I'm no saint. I've been divorced twice, but I have never slept with a married man. I could never do that. But I guess some of these other women have no scruples."

"I feel the same way. And I've seen so much of it when I was part of the Mad Men scene in New York."

"Exactly. Now go and enjoy your holiday with your wonderful wife and don't ever take her for granted."

Chapter 35

Knee-Jerk Reaction

Following the holiday weekend, everyone returned to work to find another all-employee memo from Dick Nichols. He was announcing a new task force to preempt anticipated harmful legislation that may be introduced when the Legislature convenes in January. Participants on this blue-ribbon committee would be announced shortly.

Coincidentally, Wendy Ketler and Dave had been meeting occasionally to discuss any pending legislation, where there might be unintended consequences. Their plan was if anything emerged, they could be prepared, and counter it with a public information program. But they had uncovered nothing of significance to date.

After getting the memo, Dave called Bruce Dane at the ad agency and asked him if there was any political activity going on that would impact RIHIP. Bruce had been Chief of Staff for one of the previous governors, so he was well connected to both political parties. His partner, John Marchese was a registered lobbyist and the agency provided legislative services to its clients on an as needed basis. Bruce had no information on any potential issues at the legislature.

About a week later Dave got an invitation from Nichols' secretary to attend the opening meeting of the Corporate Crisis Communications Committee in the boardroom at ten the next morning.

He arrived a little early and took a seat around the huge table as a couple of the maintenance workers were bringing in more chairs. By the time Dick called the meeting to order, there were well over forty people sitting two deep around the table. Dave was surprised to see Bruce Dane and John Marchese there, as he wasn't aware that they were invited. He also noticed Joan's absence, although Wendy Ketler was seated near Dick. Next to him were Phil Lyons and his lobbying team. Many of the attendees were outside consultants, lobbyists, and attorneys from the company's in-house legal department and their corporate law firm. Dave sat there amazed at the firepower. And wondered what this exercise was costing the firm per hour.

Sitting at one end of the long oval table, Dick had a smug look on his face, which was unusual for him. He opened the meeting and explained that he had inside knowledge that some political heavyweights in the state were planning to push legislation that would make RIHIP function more as a tightly regulated utility than an independent insurance company. "We have powerful enemies in this state, and they want to control everything about RIHIP. Their ultimate goal is to have our company become a state agency, providing health coverage to every citizen. This is the most critical challenge to our survival in RIHIP's history. And it comes when we are weakened by the erosion of our subscriber base, with losses in the tens of millions of dollars."

Dick paused for effect and then continued, "I have just elevated Phil Lyons to Executive Vice President. He and his team will spearhead the effort in the legislature, while everyone in this room will be charged with a task to beat back this attempt to take over our company."

Looking around the room, Dave observed that Dick's announcement took everyone by surprise. No one seemed to be aware of this threat to its existence as an independent company. Questions began coming from people around the table, mostly asking for names of who is leading this charge against the firm. Dick was very evasive, saying that he didn't want to share that information just yet. He did mention Mary McConnell, the outspoken head of the Department of Health, who seemed to blame RIHIP for every health issue that emerged in the state. Everyone recognized this example as a smokescreen. She was a political appointee, without any real power. Her goal had always been to get the insurers to offer more benefits without additional cost, as well as to perpetuate her job.

The meeting droned on for another hour without anything of substance coming to the table. Dick ended the meeting by saying that the group would meet each week at this time. And he commented that anyone who thought they could challenge RIHIP would be in for the fight of their lives.

Dave walked back to his office with his head swimming.

There's something else going on here. Dick didn't convince anyone there was an actual threat, although all the outside lobbyists and consultants played it up. They all saw money flowing into their coffers. I'm thankful the cost of this boondoggle is not coming out of

my budget, but it will affect the firm's profitability we're
working so hard to achieve. It's making me nervous.

Chapter 36

Spelling Bee

From   Dave Powers
To   Marcomm Mail Group
Subject Grammer Lesson

Late yesterday I was reviewing a lengthy document from an outside source, when I came across the phrase, "RIHIP will reach them in their homes, at work, and where they conjugate."

At first, I thought it was a grammetical error, but then I realized the writer was using the phrase genetically. (I'm withholding the name to protect the insolent.)

Doesn't it boggel your mind when people fracture our language like that? I just can't consummate how people could be so dents.

From   Eric Wilson
To   Marcomm Mail Group
Subject Re: Grammer Lesson

I think our boss is getting dents in his mind. Is it the water that comes from that secret spring in Maine? A couple of the staff members have noticed that he's been increasing his consumption lately. Maybe the moose herds really do use it as a toilet.

Chapter 37

Speaking While Wearing Blinders

Joan arrived at the office late on a Tuesday morning and missed the Senior Staff meeting. When Dick got out of the meeting, he had his secretary to call Joan's secretary and have her come to his office as soon as she arrived.

Joan walked in Dick's office just after 11:30 and asked Dick why he wanted to see her.

"Why weren't you at today's meeting? You should never miss one of these important meetings."

Before answering Joan thought, *and why were you rarely at these 'important' meetings when you were EVP?* But she explained, "I was meeting with a broker to work through details of landing a major employer's health insurance account."

"And that's another issue I want to talk to you about. Why are we paying these brokers so much money? We have an excellent sales staff. They are loyal and have been here their entire careers."

"They may be loyal, but they can't sell. They are order takers and provide sales and customer support."

"That's bullshit! Before you brought in this broker program, they brought in all the accounts we had."

"And we were on the verge of bankruptcy. My brokers and my marketing efforts are what's turning this company around and bringing us back to profitability."

"More bullshit. We had hit a speed bump, that's all. Once I got the computer systems upgraded, sales began to pick up. We would have been back on top without paying these brokers all that commission money. What a waste."

"Listen, Dick. You're in charge of this company, all of it. Not just Operations. Take the time to find out what's really making us successful. No one, I mean no one is buying health insurance because we have a faster running mainframe. Now, I've got calls to make." And she got up and marched out of Dick's office.

Chapter 38

What Award?

The phone call came in from one of Dave's contacts at the Health Insurance Association in Chicago. "Dave, congratulations on your big award. I'm thrilled that you won. But why weren't you and your CEO at the annual meeting? The president of the association was planning on presenting you both the plaque and the check at the banquet on Saturday night. In fact, he specifically mentioned your name when he announced the winner. He had wanted both of you to come up on stage and receive the award."

"Wait a second, Jeff. What award are we talking about? I'm not aware that we won anything, and I didn't even know about the annual meeting. This must have all been communicated directly to our CEO, Dick Nichols."

"You're kidding. Rhode Island Health Insurance Partners, the smallest member of the association from the smallest state in the Union just won the National Brand Excellence Award. And it includes a $10,000 cash prize!"

"I'm sorry Jeff. I can't believe we won. I've heard nothing about the award. Let me find out what's going on, and I'll call you back."

Dave immediately called Joan and asked about the award, but she knew nothing about it, or about Dave attending the conference to accept the prize. She was aware that Dick was going to Chicago for a meeting, but he made no mention of what it was about and what took place. She said, "My secretary is best friends with Dick's assistant Louise. Let me see what I can find out."

That afternoon Joan called Dave and shared what she learned. An invitation letter had come to Dick's office requesting his presence at the function. It also included an invite for Dave Powers, since he was the Brand Officer and had submitted the branding report that was used to determine the winner.

It turns out that Louise booked two tickets to Chicago and reserved two adjoining rooms at the Omni Hotel, ostensibly for attendance at the annual meeting. Joan described the tryst as, "So it looks like, instead of you going, Louise went to Chicago where she could participate in a *Dickathon.* Ha, ha."

Joan went on to say that she barged into Dick's office and asked about the award. She told him that she heard about the recognition from one of her contacts at the association. Dick's response was, "It's really no big deal. After all, we're in the insurance business, not in the awards business. Although I must say, the ten grand was a nice surprise. I deposited it in the general account."

"But Dick, don't you think you should make an announcement. It's a great tribute to the company. And what about recognizing Dave Powers? He works so hard to improve our brand. It has made a big difference in regaining so many of those lost subscribers."

"That's nonsense, Joan. Branding has nothing to do with it. Everybody in the state knows who we are. There's no reason to single him out for any praise."

Joan explained this to Dave and why she was so frustrated. She also realized that her making an announcement about the award at the Senior Staff would counter Dick's position, and that would only hurt Dave in the long run. So, she decided to send out a broadcast email to the entire Sales Department and include Corporate Communications.

The next day Lyons' secretary happened to see a copy of the memo and shared it with Phil. And he immediately ran down to Dick's office and showed it to him. You could feel the building shake, like a Magnitude 9.5 earthquake, and everyone sat there waiting for the aftershock that was building steam.

Chapter 39

Now There's an Idea

The next Quad-C meeting included all the same attendees as the first meeting. Dick led the meeting off with a rambling diatribe about the pending political threats to the company's independence. When he finished his monologue, there was a brief silence. Dave stepped into that void and offered a suggestion, "Why don't we launch an educational program to the entire state, so the public better understands how we help them. We do have a positive story to tell. We could expand our wellness program . . ."

Before he could continue, Dick interrupted him, saying, "That won't work. We need to take action."

Bruce Dane then spoke up and said, "Dick, I think we need to do some research of all the population segments, learn their health care apprehensions, and run a program that addresses those concerns."

Dick bellowed, "Now there's an idea. We could teach them how RIHIP's wellness program makes their lives better. That's the kind of action I'm talking about. Bruce, you outline the program and present it at the next meeting."

After a brief discussion of Bruce's concept, Dick asked one of the lobbyists, "Have you heard anything negative coming from Mary McConnell's office, the Director of Department of Health? She's one of the key players that are out to get us. She advocates free health coverage for low-income people."

"I wouldn't worry about her, Dick. She has no support for that kind of program, and she's using that position just to get media attention."

The meeting broke up shortly after that, and Dave walked back to his office wondering why Dick was spending all this money on a grandstand play that had no compelling reason for its existence. But he smiled thinking about how his wellness concept quickly became Dick's directive when Bruce Dane suggested almost the identical concept he proposed.

The next morning another all-employee memo went out from Dick's office. This one explained that the early success of the Quad-C group was the reason to make it a permanent committee. However, because of the sensitivity of its deliberations, and the individuals discussed, the committee would be reduced to a handful of outside consultants, plus the in-house corporate counsel, and Phil Lyons, the legislative EVP.

Dave felt annoyed that he was being dropped from the committee, but also relieved that he didn't have to attend those boring meetings and listen to Dick pontificate endlessly.

Chapter 40

Blunt Warning

That same day Bruce called Dave and asked him to lunch. They met in the downstairs dining room at Pot au Feu. They both ordered the Crepes Lulu, saving room for the Crème Brulé, which Bruce claimed was the best in four states. It came in a soup-bowl-size portion.

Bruce began the conversation, saying, "I couldn't believe that Dick rejected your recommendation out of hand at yesterday's meeting, and quickly approved the idea when I presented it a few minutes later. But I found out right after the meeting. Dick asked me into his office, and as soon as I sat down, he said he wanted to terminate you."

Dave was shocked and responded, "I don't get it. We had been playing golf a couple of times a month since I got to Rhode Island, although we haven't played since he was named CEO. He can't have any complaints about my performance. I'm one of probably six staff members in the entire company that has received *Exceptional* reviews ever since I joined RIHIP. My department is continuously introducing groundbreaking ideas and programs. And since hiring your agency, look what we've done together."

"Dave I couldn't agree with you more. And I think that's where the problem lies. I experienced the same situation when Fred Collins became governor. He was my best friend. I ran his election campaign and became his chief of staff. Within a month, Fred's personality changed dramatically. He must have thought he had been crowned king. After that, every decision and suggestion had to be his idea, or it was doomed. And I think that's the position you are in right now. You've been too successful, and Dick's ego can't handle it.

"He's using the excuse that you don't fit into the culture here in the state, as well as within the company. I know it's nonsense, but I think I came up with a solution. During the meeting with Dick, he told me to move full speed ahead with the new program. I told him I couldn't do it without you, since nobody at RIHIP has any experience with this kind of research or a follow-up outreach program. He reluctantly agreed.

"But Dave, please be careful and don't take credit for anything that you achieve. Make everything his idea. At the same time, I will keep working on him to convince him of your value."

Walking back to the office, Dave was experiencing dejection.

All my hard work is going to be flushed away by this self-absorbed jerk. And still worse, my dream job may end. We made a huge commitment to be here, and I may get terminated.

That night he told Elisa what was taking place and the terrible quandary he was now in. She sympathetically responded, "But he has to see your value. It can only make his position stronger."

"You're not getting it. I'm colliding with his sense of omnipotence. I'm not sure how to handle this."

"Follow Bruce's recommendation and make all your concepts his ideas. Give him credit for ideas, even if he wasn't involved. Dick will come to realize that he needs your ideas to look good. In time he will realize just how much he needs you for his own success."

"For a little Italian girl from Italy, you sure know how a buffoon's mind works."

"Well, I had lots of training getting yours straightened out." She leaned over to kiss him as they both broke out laughing, making it difficult for their lips to connect.

Chapter 41

A Great Idea

Dave spent the next couple of days thinking about the research and education program and came up with a solution that would make the entire effort a blockbuster. The trick was to use the research to create a major media event. The next Tuesday morning he hung around the parking lot behind the executive building waiting for the opportunity to intercept Dick after he parked his new Mercedes SL Roadster. As Dick drove in, Dave thought, *Al always drove the same company Chevy SUV that all the sales reps, VPs, and I drive. But the king is cruising around in this new exotic car. I'm surprised he can fit his ego in it.*

Dave met him in the hallway on the way into the Senior Staff meeting. He asked Dick, as a lifelong resident, if there had ever been a major, statewide survey of the entire population? He hinted further that he was trying to come up with an effective way to handle the research segment of the new project in a way to garner publicity.

Dick responded that he couldn't remember anything of that magnitude, and abruptly turned back to his office, saying he forgot something. Back in his office, Dick immediately called Bruce Dane and told him that he thought a statewide survey of every household in the state with lots of fanfare, would be the best way to conduct the research. He also suggested that he, as CEO would be the logical spokesperson to make the appeal in radio and TV ads. Bruce responded that he loved the concept and would work on it immediately.

Following the staff meeting, Dave went back to his office and called Bruce. "Did Dick tell you about my idea for the research?"

"Actually, no. He told me about an idea that he had to do a statewide survey, with him as the spokesperson."

"Let me rephrase the question. Did Dick tell you about my idea that he had for the program?"

"OK, Dave, now I get it. I don't know how you got the message across to him, but it worked. He knows it was your idea, but he'll never admit it. And it's a brilliant concept, by the way. Why don't you come to my office this afternoon and meet with the creative team to explain how you want to implement this survey."

A relieved Dave Powers then called his wife, Elisa. "Honey, you're not going to believe how I just played Dick and got the new program launched." When he explained his maneuver, she was excited. "Now you're on the right track. You must be getting good advice from someone."

"Yes, I am. I can't remember her name, but I know she's just learning how to kiss."

Chapter 42

Into the Lyons Den

Dave was cleaning up his inbox at the end of the day, when another all-employee email came in. This one announced that the Marketing Communications Department was being transferred to the Legislative Affairs Division and would be under the direction of Phil Lyons. It would also change its name to Corporate Communications. Dave Powers, Chief Communications Officer would now be reporting directly to Phil Lyons.

In reading the document, Dave noticed that it made no mention of continuing its service to its major internal client, the Sales and Marketing Division or any of the dozens of other departments that relied on his team for their events, marketing programs, product literature, and more.

Dave quickly put in a call to Joan, but her secretary told him that she had just run down to Dick's office to *rip him a new one.* Dave left a message to return his call.

An exasperated Joan called back a little while later. She told Dave that she was as blindsided as everyone else by the announcement. The move was obviously hatched by Nichols and Lyons without any thought to how Phil was actually going to manage the department. He was such a nervous introvert that he couldn't make a coherent report at Staff meetings. How was he going to direct the communications department?

But Dick had his mind made up. There was no going back on this decision.

A short time later, Dave got a call from Lyons' secretary to come to his office immediately. That directive even further incensed Dave. Did Phil think that he sat around all day just waiting to be called into a meeting?

When Dave got to Lyons' office, his secretary had him stand there and wait as Phil was on the phone. After a ten-minute discourse on the best restaurants in Providence, Lyons ended the call, and his secretary invited him into Phil's office to sit in a chair across from Phil's desk. Without preamble or small talk, Lyons gave him his new marching orders.

"Dick has decided that your department needs more discipline and more structure. Going forward you will submit a written report to me every Monday morning on your planned weekly activities, plus the results of your previous week's efforts. You will initiate no new programs without my authorization. The current advertising campaign is to be cancelled immediately. From now on, all new advertising will be of a more traditional nature, commensurate with the professional stature of an insurance institution. All new concepts are to be approved in advance by Dick and me. In fact, Dick wants to be consulted at the beginning of the thought stage of the development process."

Lyons recited the directives as if from rote. Dave then asked, "Phil, do you know what you're talking about? Do you have any experience or knowledge of the principles of marketing, branding or mass communications? Are you familiar with media schedules, TV production, branding strategy? Do you realize we have contracts with the media regarding our advertising schedule and we cannot stop immediately without paying hundreds of thousands of dollars for ads that will not run."

"I studied all that in college, so yes, I do know what I'm talking about. And why are we be wasting hundreds of thousands of dollars on ads?"

"Let me stop you right there. Do you actually think we've been so successful these past two years because we used textbook solutions to marketing problems? Do you have any idea of how the trendsetting programs that we've implemented have completely turned the tide on our sales results? Do you really think that the staggering 20% shift in market share over the last two years happened by itself?"

"No, it didn't happen without a tremendous effort on the company's part. I got new legislation passed that enabled us to offer more policy variations, the kind of products people really want. Dick drastically updated our call center, which improved customer satisfaction. And he had the IT department install new programming to reduce billing errors, and process claims faster. That's how we have increased sales. Not with your frivolous advertising."

Standing up, Dave responded, "Oh, and how did anybody know about these changes if we didn't communicate them? There is nothing else to be said here. I will start preparing your weekly reports. And when our brand perception drops back to where it was when I arrived. And when we again become the most hated company in the state, you can tout my reports as evidence of your solution. And yes, I will cancel the ad campaign immediately. But you probably already know since you studied it in college, that once I kill the ads, we will have no replacement advertising. And we will have to pay for the ad time that we contracted with the media. Were you even awake during your marketing classes in college?" And with that, Dave got up and walked out of Lyons' Office.

Chapter 43

Sage Advice

It was Friday evening, date night for Dave and Elisa. They started the tradition of ending the workweek with a quiet dinner together when they moved into their home in Ramsey, NJ. And they've continued it after moving to Rhode Island.

They sat at a booth at the Coast Guard House in Narragansett. After a toast and a first sip of the wine, Dave began telling Elisa about his week from hell. "Lise, you can't believe the archaic thinking that I encounter from seasoned executives at this excuse for a corporation. Most of the Senior Staff members at the company would not have been able to get an entry-level position at our agency. And collectively they are running a billion-dollar enterprise with a staff of 2,000. The entire Rhode Island healthcare delivery system depends on their solvency and timely reimbursements in order to manage their cash flow. And half the residents of the state count on RIHIP's benefits to pay for their care."

After explaining his encounter with Lyons, he commented, "My dream job is over. Dick's directive is going to stifle my creativity, and together Nichols and Lyons and going to micromanage my every move. I won't be able to work in that environment. I am almost certainly going to have to leave the company."

"David, you can't leave. We rely on their insurance. And besides, once they realize the importance of your creative programs, they will back off and let you run your department without their interference."

"Lise Honey, with their tunnel vision they don't have the mental capacity to understand what I do, or how much impact it has on the company. My situation will not change here. Fortunately, I have now built a reputation in the industry with all the awards I've won and my speaking engagements at the conferences. I could easily get a job with another health insurer. But it will mean moving to another part of the country."

"Yes, that is a possibility, but then you would not be fully vested and would give up a huge amount of your 401K and retirement benefits. Please listen to me. Take it slow and move carefully. Let's see how it plays out. If it turns out we have to move, I'm okay with it being our next adventure. But first give it a little more time."

"Your soothing voice and accurate advice just lowered my temperature and my blood pressure. Thank you, Mrs. Doctor Powers."

Chapter 44

Playing the Corporate Game

Dave showed up early and fresh on Monday morning. He had thought about everything that had transpired on Friday, particularly Elisa's comments about giving up a large portion of his benefits. He decided to try to make the situation work for him. If Nichols and Lyons were determined to micromanage him, he was going to bury them in detail until they gave up and let him run his department.

He sent Lyons an email telling him that he had a solution to Dick's request to cancel the ad campaign. He requested a meeting whenever Phil had the time. He also attached a twelve-page report of ongoing activities, which he wrote over the weekend. He drafted it with as much technical jargon as he could muster, knowing that Phil wouldn't understand any of it. And he requested feedback from Lyons on each of the dozens of projects listed in the report.

At 10:45 Phil's secretary called and asked if Dave could come right over. This time Dave waited thirty minutes before leaving his office. When he arrived, she had him sit in the same chair as before, while Lyons sat behind his desk working on some paperwork. Finally, when he thought Dave got the point, he moved the sheaf of papers, and addressed him. "Dave, I told Dick about the problem of not having any commercials to run in place of the existing campaign, and he said to run the old ads from a few years ago."

"I thought of that, but we'd have to renegotiate the residuals. And that would cost a fortune. You never want to go back to the talent after the original contract."

"What are residuals?"

"Sorry, I thought you would have studied that in college. Residuals are payments made to on-air talent every time a commercial is run. You plan your flight schedule and work out pricing with the talent based on the number of spots that air. Once the contract ends, you must sign a new deal to run another flight. And the price always goes up substantially. The reason being the actors think the program was successful and they want a bigger bite."

"What a stupid process. After you pay them to appear in the commercial, why would you pay them more money every time it airs on TV? And now we have to renegotiate a new contract? Dick will never allow us to pay them again for something they did a couple of years ago. How could you sign a contract like that?"

Frustrated Dave responded, "These people are referred to as *talent* for a reason. Their acting is what makes the ads deliver results. This is standard procedure in the industry and has been for decades. We can't make our own rules in an industry this size. We simply will not be able to run the spots without paying them. But I have a better solution. Why don't you ask Dick if he'd like to appear as the company spokesperson in a series of public relations ads that talk about the benefits of RIHIP? We could run those spots in place of what he wants to cancel. And it would continue to help enhance the image of the company. Let me know what he thinks, and we'll schedule production.

"And get back to me within 48 hours with your feedback of my report. I will need to know if you plan to make changes to any of the other programs that are in production."

"How can I do that? I don't know anything about your projects."

"Then you'd better learn fast. Read my reports and start spending time in my department. Get to know the staff, since they work for you. And get to learn about the details of the programs we produce. Otherwise, how can you ever manage the department?"

Phil stared at him incredulously, "How can I do that. I have my own department to run."

"But now this is also your department. Please understand that responsibility comes with this added power. There is no free lunch."

"I don't have the time to oversee what you're doing. I have important work to do."

"I manage eight times the number of people you do, so I'm just as busy as you, probably a lot busier. And it is just as important. From now on, don't expect me to jump every time you want to see me. Give me some advance notice or wait until I can break from my busy schedule."

Chapter 45

Shrinking Responsibility

The next morning, Dave got a call from Lyons' secretary asking him to come right over. Dave answered, "I'm in a meeting. I'll get there when I can."

When he got to Phil's office at 11 am, he said, "As I told you yesterday, I don't sit around waiting for you to call. I manage twenty-five people and we do real work. So, either make an appointment or give me a time range when you'll be available."

Visibly annoyed, Lyons told him that Dick wanted to go ahead with the new commercials, except he didn't want to promote RIHIP products, but talk about how the company contributes to the wellness of the Rhode Island residents.

Lyons also said, "I ran into Jack Landrieu at the state house, and he suggested that the quantity of the prescription bag orders be doubled but produced less often, as a way to overcome the new price increase on the bag production. Landrieu explained that the pharmacies were increasing their requests, and the reorders were becoming more frequent." Dave agreed that printing the larger quantity, less frequently made more sense.

Dave left Lyons office feeling very good about the meeting. His recommendation to use Dick in the campaign worked. He knew that if he had suggested all the details of the new commercials, it would have been rejected. But by letting Dick modify the concept, he would own it, and Dave was able to get what he wanted. He also felt good about putting Lyons in his place and not expecting him to jump when he beckoned.

It was a shame that he had to play these mind games just to get any serious concept approved. But that is what he was learning about dealing with the corporate bureaucracy under Nichols' tyrannical reign of egotism. He also learned that bureaucrats are not prepared for pushback, and he planned to use it more.

When he got back to the office, Dave called the ad agency and told them about the new campaign. He wanted to get it scheduled for production immediately.

While he was on the phone, Bruce told him he had the details of the new statewide research project ready. He planned to come over to Dave's office later that day to present the plan. Dave explained that once he approved it, he would take it to Lyons to get Dick's approval. And he was certain that Dick would want to bring it to the new, smaller size Quad-C group and share the program with them and boast about the details of the wonderful concept he thought up.

Bruce commented, "It was certainly a lot easier when you could make the final decision and we could get right into production."

"Bruce, I think those days are gone forever. And so are the days of developing breakthrough marketing programs."

Chapter 46

Only One Take

Dave sent six scripts to Lyons for him to get approval from Dick. He knew that Nichols would reject two or three of them, but all he wanted was three finished ads. Not unexpectedly, Dick rejected all six and decided to write his own text. He wanted the messages to be personalized using his own words.

In the meantime, Dave had the agency schedule the shoot. On the morning of the taping, Dave still did not have Dick's revised scripts. He called Lyons and explained that the shoot was in two hours, and they would be charged for any delays. The studio needed the scripts right away to set up the teleprompter.

Dick's drafts were complete an hour later, and he forwarded them directly to the agency. Dave then left for the studio to oversee all aspects of the video shoot.

Despite being advised to arrive a half-hour early for make-up, Dick showed up at exactly 11 o'clock. He was rushed through his make-up and prep and then positioned in front of the camera. While Dick was getting ready, Dave made a couple of grammatical edits to the scripts. He also had to cut the copy as every script ran well over the 60 second maximum. And once that was completed, he handed them off and got the teleprompter set up.

When the crew was ready to shoot, Dick announced that he was not going to use the scripts on the teleprompter. He decided that he would let the message flow as he spoke. Recognizing the danger in this directive, Dave politely suggested to Dick that they shoot the scripts as written, and then reshoot them however he wanted to deliver them. And then in post-production, they can edit different phrases and sentences in and out. Dick rejected that idea out of hand, saying, "Look, I don't have time to stand in front of the camera all day. We're doing one take of each of the six scripts. Period."

Although Dave was concerned, he wasn't too worried. Dick had lots of experience speaking in front of large crowds, and they only needed three of the six scripts for the campaign. But the unexpected happened. Sometimes people, who are comfortable speaking to an audience, panic when there is a camera pointed at them. It's the same feeling as staring down the barrel of a shotgun when you know your girlfriend is pregnant.

Dick was visibly awkward delivering his lines. He also wandered way off script, sliding into colloquialisms and poor grammar. And he ran over time on every single spot. And with a self-satisfied smile he said to the cameraman, "They should be perfect, I nailed it."

With that remark, he stepped away from the screen, and prepared to leave. Dave stopped him and said, "Dick we have to reshoot these spots, they are all over the sixty-second time, and there are too many syntax errors."

Dick's nervous energy and Dave's disheartening comment caused an internal safety valve to blow, and he shouted at Dave, "I told you one take. Fix the damn timing in the studio. And those weren't errors. It's how we speak in Rhode Island. But you wouldn't understand that since you're from *Brooklyn*." And with that, he turned and stormed out.

Dave spent the next two and a half days working with the sound technician and video editor to salvage three commercials. While he was able to edit them down to sixty seconds, he couldn't hide Dick's uncomfortable expression and poor grammar. And all the extra postproduction time raised the costs to double the original budget. Yet despite the huge cost overrun, the commercials were still awful. Reluctantly, he had the files sent to Lyons for Dick to approve.

Chapter 47

Maybe a Second Take?

Around noon on Monday, Lyons called him and told him that Dick really liked the finals. And he advised Dave to remove the existing campaign and plug in Dick's messages. That night on the six o'clock news the first spot ran, and people were horrified. Some just laughed, but other concerned viewers, including a few insurance brokers, employees, and even Dick's brother called the RIHIP call center and left messages about the ads. They all urged RIHIP to drop the campaign immediately.

At Senior Staff the next morning, before anyone could comment on the campaign, Dick addressed the team. "Before any of you say anything, we are removing those terrible commercials. I can't believe Powers approved them to run."

Dave overreacted to the obvious lie, and responded, "Dick, Let's get the story straight. I warned you about those spots and even sent them to you to approve."

"That's bullshit! I never saw them. Now take them down and run the previous campaign until I can figure out what to do next."

Dave realized that his kneejerk response was a fatal mistake, and he never should have contradicted Dick in front of all the company's executives. He had done irreparable damage to his already diminished relationship with Dick. And his defensive reaction all but convinced the staff that he was the one who screwed up.

When the meeting ended, not one person came over to him. In fact, everyone gave him a wide berth as they left the boardroom.

Chapter 48

Golf Musings

Dave and Elisa played golf that weekend at a golf course just over the state line in Connecticut. It was a scenic track, but the conditions were not very favorable. It was also a tight course, due to the fact that there wasn't enough acreage to spread the holes out properly. After golf, they drove down to the waterfront and had dinner at a casual, dockside restaurant.

As they sipped wine, waiting for their entrees, they talked about the round of golf. Dave commented that the course was somewhat disappointing as were many of the courses they had been playing in the area. Comparing it with other courses they've played, he observed, "Rhode Island is such a beautiful state, but its golf courses don't come up to the level of the courses we used to play in New Jersey and New York. Even the private clubs, with a few exceptions, fall below the level of private country clubs in other states."

"You're right, David. The golf courses in this area are not manicured and elegant like many of the clubs we've been to."

"The other thing I noticed is that there are almost no gated, residential golf communities in Rhode Island."

Following their early dinner, they drove around Westerly before heading back home to East Greenwich. As they cruised around, Dave noted, "There's still a lot of vacant land here in the Westerly/Hopkinton area. This would be a great location to build a gated golf community."

"David, what are you saying? You want to build a golf course?"

"Oh, I would love to, but I'm merely dreaming. We certainly don't have the resources to undertake a project like that."

Surprised by his response, she probed further, "Would you even consider leaving RIHIP, given our health insurance issue with my breast cancer? And would you even remotely consider an undertaking of that magnitude? This is not like the spec houses we built in New Jersey. This would be a multi-year multimillion dollar project."

"Lise, regarding the insurance concern, in one more year you will be five years cancer-free. We will again be eligible for insurance without the pre-existing condition barrier. And as I said, I'm just musing."

Chapter 49

Beware the Ghosts

Without any fanfare, the healthcare questionnaire was mailed to every household in Rhode Island. It was the largest survey ever distributed by mail in the history of the state. And as planned, it got the attention of everyone. The news media began calling RIHIP to find out more about the cost and the expected results of this ambitious program.

In his department's staff meeting that morning, Dave explained the strategy of the program. "We deliberately did not announce this survey to the press. If we had, there would have been a *ho-hum* response. So instead, we sprung it on the population to create a buzz, and now everyone will be talking about it. The survey is designed to elicit responses that will tell us what the residents of the state want in their health insurance policies; what additional benefits they are willing to pay for; and what features they could do without. There are also questions about wellness and fitness, and it probes them about end-of-life issues."

Eric noted, "There was nothing in this morning's newspaper about the mailing." Others nodded.

Dave continued, "The survey is only the opening salvo. We are also going to launch a huge study, which is already underway, that will offer better solutions to health and longevity without bankrupting the population. That's what the program is all about. At the end of the day, every person in the state will have much more respect and admiration for RIHIP. And that's how you take the fictional fangs out of the imaginary legislators that want to take control of RIHIP and the health delivery system in Rhode Island."

That brought laughter from the team.

"We're going to announce a press conference in the next couple of days to explain the program to the public."

It was Shari Wolfson who spoke up. "Is there really a move by the State to take over the company? I know in Vermont, the legislature controls Blue Cross, which is about the only serious health insurer there. My husband works in the governor's office, and he told me that he's certain that a takeover move is not on anyone's agenda."

"Shari, I feel the same way. But when you live in a world that knows no reality, you have nightmares about monsters under the bed. And this person I refer to, sleeps on a really wide bed that can hide all the state legislators under it. We are paying $1 million to *The Ghostbusters* to clean up that bedroom. It will be interesting to learn what other ghosts reside there."

The room went quiet. And when everyone saw the smirk on Dave's face, they all broke out laughing again.

Later in the day, Dave called Bruce, and discussed the press conference that they had been planning. "Every reporter in the state, and many others from as far away as Boston are calling to find out what this survey is all about. We should schedule the conference for later this week."

I agree, Dave. I have prepared Dick Nichols' remarks and your talking points, but I think we should get Dick in here for some media training before he gets in front of the camera."

"I agree. In fact, I'll take advantage of the offer for coaching myself. Although I'm comfortable speaking in public, I'm a little rusty answering questions being fired at me by the press. I'll call Dick's office and see what time this afternoon he can make it."

Dave emailed Dick's remarks to his secretary and called her to schedule Dick for the training. She called back shortly, and told Dave that Dick was going to make a few edits to the brief speech and was declining the training session. She told Dave that he would have no problem delivering the few remarks without any coaching.

Shooting from the Lip

Kathy Cormier, the event planner for RIHIP supervised the set up for the press conference in the small ballroom of the Biltmore Hotel. There were several chairs set up behind a lectern on the podium at the front of the room. And coffee and pastries were put out in the back for the attendees.

In a small dressing room off the ballroom, Dave went over all the details and was prepared to deliver his remarks after Dick's introductory statement. Also in the room were Kathy, Bruce Dane, and Dick who was pacing nervously as he reread his brief speech. Not unexpectedly, Phil Lyons showed up late and got there just before the conference was scheduled to start. And although he had no active part in the presentation, he looked more anxious that Dick.

Dick looked at Dave and remarked, "Why are you so calm with all those vultures out there waiting to tear into us?"

"Relax, Dick. When you're prepared, public speaking is easy. Just channel your nervousness and read your lines. Everyone likes you, so smile and use your charm. I'll be giving the details, so I'm the one who will be on the firing line."

When it was time, the five of them walked up to the podium and took their seats. Kathy walked up to the lectern, positioned her mike a little lower, and looked out at the crowd that was gathered. There were TV cameras from seven stations, including two from Boston, over a dozen microphones, plus reporters, technicians and some RIHIP executives that brought the audience to about fifty people. The confined space gave the appearance of the room being crowded, which was Dave's intent.

Kathy welcomed everyone and introduced Richard F. Nichols, President and CEO of Rhode Island Health Insurance Partners.

Dick stood, gave his best smile, strutted up to the front of the podium and placed his text on the stand. When he looked up at the cameras and the press attendees, he faltered. Recovering, he began to read his speech, "Good morning everyone and thank you for coming. As president and CEO of Rhode Island Health Insurance Partners, I'm pleased to announce that RIHIP is undertaking an important study to improve the health care delivery system and the wellness of the residents in Rhode Island. This program will reduce insurance costs while making people healthier."

Before Dick could close with his final comment, the reporters all interrupted him with questions.

"Why is RIHIP doing this survey, and not the health care community?"

"Was it necessary to mail a multi-page survey to every household in the state?"

"What is this boondoggle costing? The postage alone must be over a quarter of a million dollars."

"If you're so concerned about everyone's health, why do you deny coverage, and refuse to pay for certain treatments?"

The questions were coming from every corner of the room, and Dick was overwhelmed. Noticeably shaken he put his hands up and stated that Dave Powers would provide more details and answer their questions. With that, he sat down with an angry scowl on his face.

Although Dick was supposed to introduce Dave, Kathy quickly jumped up and made the introduction.

Dave got up and calmly addressed the audience without referring to any notes. During his talk, he worked in the responses to the questions that had been asked earlier. He explained that RIHIP wanted to hear from everyone in the state, and not just do a sample interview. They opted to use mail to get accurate, detailed responses. And after careful review with various consultants, the company's management determined that it was worth the cost, because the benefit would affect the entire state population over the long-term.

Dave then went on to describe the in-depth study that would take place following the completion of the survey. Representatives of the hospitals, physician groups, pharmaceutical manufacturers, and even Brown University's medical school would all be studying the data and making recommendations to the report that would be delivered.

By the end of his comments, all their concerns had been addressed. There were a few softball questions, and the conference ended.

Back in the dressing room, Dick came up to Dave and said, "That was the worst disaster I've ever experienced." And with that he charged out of the room.

Right after lunch, Elisa called Dave and told him how proud she was of her brilliant husband. He laughed and said, "Oh, Hi, Mrs. Nichols. Dick did a great job, didn't he?"

"I'm Elisa Powers, and *my* husband was the one who did a great job. The press was eating out of his hand,"

"What's with all the flattery? Is there something expensive you are looking to buy for yourself?"

"David, did you watch the 12 o'clock news? Dick looked like an arrogant fool. He had to *read* that short spiel from his notes, which made him look insincere, and the press skewered him. So instead of answering their questions, he gets pissed off and hands it off to you. And you were great! The best part was as he was sitting on the podium, he was still on camera. His facial expressions and body language just made him look worse. And the cameras made sure they gave him plenty of facetime."

"He deserved all he got, the arrogant fool. Unfortunately, I didn't see any of it."

"Oh, and when did I ever have to kiss up to you if I wanted to buy something extravagant?"

"You never buy anything extravagant."

Chapter 51

The Investors

Using some vacation days, Dave and Elisa went to New Jersey for a long weekend. They spent most of their time visiting friends, but Dave took off Saturday to play golf at the exclusive North Jersey Country Club, as a guest of Elisa's cousin, Leo Cantelmo. Leo was a very successful industrialist, having founded a large chemical company in Passaic. Although short in stature, he was a high energy, aggressive individual, with a golfer's tan and a likeable, generous personality.

During the round, Leo commented to Dave, "Elisa told my wife that you are considering building a golf community. Are you serious about this idea?"

"Well, I can't say I'm serious, but we did have a couple of conversations about it. There are very few residential golf communities in Rhode Island, so there is a strong need to develop one. In fact, we uncovered an incredible site that has several moneymaking options. But I don't have the capital to undertake anything of that size."

"Let's talk more after golf. I'm very intrigued by this concept."

Following the round, they went into the clubhouse for a drink. Waiting there for Leo was a friend of his, who Leo introduced. "Dave, this is Ernie Pagano. I texted him from the course and told him to meet us. You see, Ernie and I have been doing some real estate deals in New York, and we've been talking about a golf course for a few years now. Let's have a drink so you can tell us what you're thinking."

After ordering a mojito, Dave explained his concept, "Traveling around Rhode Island, and playing golf at just about every public and private course, I recognized that there would be a demand for a luxury gated golf community, particularly in the southern part of the state.

My idea is to build a resort-style community with condos, private homes, and a hotel. The reason for the hotel is that there are very few hotels between Interstate 95 in Rhode Island and the southern beaches along its shoreline. The course would be open to the hotel guests, and to the residents of the community. There would also be limited access to outside play for guests at the Connecticut casinos, since they have no golf courses. The casino owners really need entree to a quality golf course, as their guests are clamoring for it."

Ernie turned to Leo and said, "This sounds very interesting." Leo smiled and nodded.

"Now please understand that I have no experience to build such a facility, but I have built several homes in the million-dollar range, including my former residence in Ramsey. And during the last recession, I sold a spec home in Upper Saddle River that I built, for over $1 million. In Rhode Island, I manage a major department with a $7 million budget. I know how to get things done, even big projects."

As Dave talked, Ernie was becoming excited by what he was hearing. He asked, "Dave, do you think that you could put together the resources to build that kind of development in Rhode Island, if we put up the money?"

"To answer your question, I have the organizational skills and the contacts there to put a team together. I also have some political connections through my position at Rhode Island Health Insurance Partners. But please keep in mind we are a long way from doing anything of that magnitude at this time."

Leo said, "I like the fact that you have some political clout. And we get that this would take time, but is it feasible?"

"I'm aware of some vacant land that may be available, but I don't know at what price. And I have no idea of any wetland issues with any of these parcels. I know a few builders, law firms, and a restaurateur that could run the clubhouse and the catering facility.

"For me, this has been a creative exercise. Up until now, I've just been dreaming about it, and have not considered it seriously. I just don't have the capital. But if the two of you are serious, I will check out the land first. If it's viable, then you come up and take a look. I will then talk to the lawyers. And if they're comfortable with the concept, we can move forward from there."

Leo answered for the two of them. "We are very serious, but let's keep this between us for the time being. Do your research and call me."

Chapter 52

Not My Fault

Joan called Dave at his office early Monday morning. "Dave, I'm still home, but I wanted to talk to you before I got to the office this morning. While you were out Friday, Dick was going around complaining about the press conference. He told most of the executives on the floor that you screwed it up, and didn't give him the right talking points, and didn't prepare him for what happened. Is that possible?"

"Joan, that is the purest horseshit money can buy, fresh from the horse's ass. He had the same prep notes that I had. And I arranged for him to get media training before the event, just like I received. He's the CEO. Shouldn't he know the answers, even without notes? I didn't have any trouble, and if his ego wasn't in the way, neither would he. Maybe this will be a wake-up call for him. I really know what I'm doing, and if he would just listen to me, he'd get it. What did I do to turn him off like this?"

"It's not you, it's your success that troubles him. He wants all the glory. And you showing him up at the press conference is just one more nail in the coffin. It just made matters that much worse."

"People who watched the press conference have told me how bad he looked on TV. I can't help him if he's too proud to do what is needed."

"Dick's been treating everyone, including all of us on Senior Staff as inferior subjects of the kingdom. And all he talks about is his Quad-C war room meetings, and how we're going to bring the legislature and all the state agencies to their knees. This obsession is really getting tired and it's becoming impossible to work with him. I can tell that failure is on the horizon if he can't get focused on the business rather than the legislature."

Chapter 53

The Dream Takes Shape

That night over dinner, Dave told Elisa about his weekend conversation with her cousin's husband Leo and with his talk that morning with Joan. "Lise, the ground is shifting under us, and we have to reconsider our situation. My job with RIHIP is getting tenuous, and I'm afraid that Dick may fire me at any time."

"What? RIHIP doesn't fire anyone. You didn't strangle Phil Lyons in one of the hallways, did you? What's going on?"

"Apparently, Dick has a particular dislike for me. I'm told it's because of my successful track record, but the press conference last week, really pissed him off, and he's blaming me for his bad showing."

"But David, you must find a way to make it work. We agreed that it would be too costly to leave now. And the insurance problem scares me."

"That's a non-issue. I spoke to one of the actuaries, and he confirmed to me that after five years, it's no longer a pre-existing condition that will deny you coverage. Based on that, we really can leave anytime. If

I were to leave now, we could apply for COBRA insurance through RIHIP for 18 months. They can't deny that coverage, and that would more than cover us until your five-year anniversary.

"But understand, I'm not ready to pull the plug just yet. And I won't leave without having a position to move into. And I certainly have to get vested. If he fires me, then all bets are off."

"You're really making me nervous."

"Then let me tell you about my discussion with Leo, and later with his friend Ernie. During the golf round, we began talking about gated golf communities, and how Rhode Island could really use a luxury residential golf development. Well, I was talking casually about it, and Leo got all excited. He called Ernie, and we had drinks after golf. They grilled me on the idea and became really intrigued with investigating the concept. I told them I would do some research and get back to them."

"David, are you serious? That is much too big a project for you to handle. How could you possibly take on a development like that?"

"Lise let's take it a step at a time. They want me to research some land. I'll call our realtor, Ron Phipps and see what's available. If we find something, I'll check out any wetlands issues and then I'll bring Leo and Ernie up to walk the property."

"Oh my God. You are serious. Do you really think you could pull off something like this?"

"If you think about it, it's not that much different than what I'm doing at the office. While the disciplines are different, the management responsibility is similar. I told them that I don't have the experience on a project like this. But I know home construction, and I have the skills to coordinate the major contractors, and get it done. Wouldn't you like to live on a golf course, and manage the club?"

Chapter 54

A Clandestine Offer

Bruce Dane called a meeting at the ad agency for 9 the following morning to discuss the results of the survey and the response program. Dave attended the meeting with two of his staff members, a writer and a production manager.

Bruce led off the meeting by stating that the survey administration company had presented vastly more data than expected, due to the extremely large response from the recipients. He mentioned that the size of the response indicated the desire for change in the industry. When Dave saw the size of the paper file of information, he commented, "Bruce, why don't we translate that body of information, and produce a massive report that we can present to all our constituent audiences, including the governor, the legislators, the healthcare-related agencies, and others."

"Dave I was thinking along the same lines, except we should also preview it with the healthcare entities for their input and inclusion in the report. Let's have your department start writing the document. I will have our art department design the graphics, and we'll move quickly to completion. This could be a blockbuster deliverable!"

After the lengthy meeting, Dave left the agency and went directly to The Capital Grill to meet Jack Landrieu. Jack had called him early that morning to say he had good news and wanted to meet for lunch.

They both arrived about the same time, and as soon as they sat down, Jack handed Dave two more letters from local pharmacies. Similar to the original letter he had given Dave at the beginning of the program, these were copies of letters thanking RIHIP for their continuing generosity by providing the prescription bags at no charge.

A little later in the discussion, Jack invited Dave to play golf at his club the following weekend. Dave accepted and thanked him. And he asked a seemingly odd question, "Jack is there any possibility your club would consider building homes around the course? There's some vacant land, and a lot of clubs are considering this opportunity to raise funds."

"Interesting you should ask that. We recently looked into that option, but the land just isn't suitable for home construction. There is too much bedrock that would require blasting, and the low areas are all wetlands. The combination is too much to overcome. But why do you ask?"

"Some friends from New Jersey are considering building a gated golf course community in the state. And I offered to do some early-stage research for them." Dave was deliberately coy on sharing too many details.

With that, Jack became much more attentive. "Dave, the only feasible place for that kind of development is South County. You don't have the ledgestone formations down there, but there is always the wetlands issue. Rhode Island is very strict about infringement.

"If you locate the right parcel of land, let me know. I would like to meet your associates. And if you go forward, I can help you navigate the process. You see, I was instrumental in appointing the Director of Environmental Management. If you encounter and questionable wetlands, he will respond to my intercession. I also do some consulting for companies looking to locate in the state. For a project like yours, my involvement will facilitate a smooth approval and oversight process. And that's often very difficult in a state like ours, especially for outsiders."

"Thank you, Jack. If they move forward, I will definitely make the introduction."

Dave left the restaurant with his head spinning from the exchange about the land issues, and by Jack jumping on the opportunity to get involved. He wondered if he had said too much. Dave recognized that if the project did go forward, he would almost certainly need some *inside help*. But he also had trepidations about even the perception of something that could be construed as bribery.

Chapter 55

Misplaced Praise

Returning to the office, Dave sent the pharmacists thank you letters to Phil Lyons with a note to share them with Dick, Wendy, and the other executives. Dave immediately got a strong email from Lyons telling him to have no more contact with Jack Landrieu. The memo directed Dave that going forward, Phil and his staff would work directly with him and all the legislators on current and future projects.

This fit Dave's plan as he had decided that he didn't want to take any more credit for the continued success of the program. No doubt Dick would now take ownership of the project and boast about his idea to put RIHIP prescription bags in the independent pharmacies.

Sure enough, the next morning an all-employee memo went out with copies of the letters, and praise for Phil Lyons and the Legislative Affairs Department for implementing *his* innovative concept. He ended the email with the comment, "Now this is how you run a first-class department." Fortunately for Dave, his name was not mentioned in the memo.

That afternoon, he met with his staff and told them about the new phase of the survey and report program. Walking back from lunch, he had come up with an appropriate name for the new segment. He suggested *Project Insight* to his team, and they all liked it. He also asked them to think of other titles and share them.

Just before he left the office, he got a call from Ron Phipps the realtor. Dave, I'm sending some property descriptions to your home email. I'm excited about their potential. I think they will be perfect for your project." He also made an appointment to pick Dave up at his house at 9 on Saturday morning to look at this land in South County.

Driving home on that Friday afternoon, Dave thought about his hectic week at the office.

This survey project is building up to a dramatic conclusion that would become one of my all-time best campaigns with national implications. And the bag program is performing better than I expected. But it's all so frustrating as I am going nowhere in this company. I can't believe how my fortunes have changed a full 180 degrees.

This golf course project is getting me excited, but it's still a pipe dream. Too much must come together for it to become a reality. But I need something to change my direction.

Chapter 56

All About the Timing

The public service announcements featuring Adam Vinatieri had been running for several months and early in the program, Dave had arranged for Adam to make appearances and speak at a handful of grade school and high school events. The program was enjoying excellent awareness among kids of all ages.

With the ads in full swing, Wendy Ketler called Dave one morning with an idea. "Dave, one of the nursing advisors suggested we run an essay contest among the Rhode Island students and offer a scholarship for the best submission.

"What a great idea. We could do categories for grade school, middle school, and high school. And we can give grants in each category. I'll get Adam to record a TV commercial and use it to promote the contest."

Wendy was getting very excited. "Yes. I'll leave it to you to put it together. This will be a home run!"

"No Wendy, wrong sport. It will be a touchdown."

Dave's staff put the program together and got it ready for launch. He called Adam and asked if he could record a commercial on his day off. "I'll sweeten my request for your recording time by taking you and Mrs. Vinatieri out to dinner with my wife, Elisa and me. And maybe even throw in a round of golf."

Laughing, Adam answered, "I can do it next Monday. Dinner sounds like fun. And golf. Now you're talking."

The program kicked off and it got enthusiastic responses at all age levels. The two couples met and enjoyed dinner at the Capital Grill. When they played golf, Adam outdrove Dave on every hole by fifty yards or more, but Dave's score was four strokes lower.

When the contest deadline arrived, over twenty-thousand essays had been submitted. Dave insisted that every student receive a Certificate of Participation, with printed signatures of Wendy and Adam.

Three scholarships in each age category were awarded at a ceremony on the steps of RIHIP headquarters. Adam and Wendy presented the awards in front of the TV cameras of all the area stations.

Dick had been playing golf that afternoon and was not aware of the presentation. When he saw it on the TV news that night, he flung his newspaper at the TV. "What the hell is that?" he shouted at no one. "Must be one of Power's bullshit programs."

The next morning, he had Wendy in his office reaming her out. "Did you authorize that waste of money I saw on TV last night? I'll bet it was one of Powers' stupid ideas."

"It was a brilliant idea, and it came from my department. Twenty-three thousand families participated, and we've been getting press coverage for months. Why are you so negative?"

Chapter 57

A Nice Piece of Dirt

Dressed in jeans and hiking boots, Dave and Ron headed south to a farm on Route 3 in Hopkinton. Ron knew the owner, a widow in her late sixties, who had run the farm for twenty years after her husband passed until she shut it down recently. She invited them into her weather-beaten home, which was badly in need of repair and paint. They sat in the dining room at a huge trestle table that was easily 50 years older than her. She was thin and frail with unkempt gray hair and dark penetrating eyes. Although she looked and dressed like an aging farmer, she proved to be a savvy woman with a hard edge, who knew her way around real estate and the local politics. The first question she asked was, "Do you work for the casinos?"

Surprised at the question, Dave assured her that this was a project he would own, along with some investors from Rhode Island and New Jersey. That didn't completely convince her, so she added, "If I decide to sell you the land, and my neighbors go in on the sale with their land, there will be a clause in the sales contract that will state that if you are connected

154

in any way to the Indian tribes, their management company, or the casinos, the sale will be cancelled and you will forfeit any and all deposits, payments, or escrow balances."

"Believe me, I have no intention of partnering with the tribes."

"Mr. Powers, my neighbors and I are very serious about this caveat. We want nothing to do with their filthy money. And worse than losing your money, if I find out you're lying to me, I'll fill your ass with buckshot." Ron sat there stone-faced, but seeing Dave's smirk, she added, "Mr. Powers, I am dead serious about that."

Following her tirade, they discussed the land and the pricing. She also spoke for the three neighbor's parcels that would be needed to provide enough acreage for the development.

Ron and Dave left her home and walked around the property, which was a combination of rolling hills and sloping pastures. Taking some photos, Dave recognized that it would be an excellent setting for the golf course, by providing variations in the terrain, and lots of open space to build the housing. The four parcels would total out to about six hundred acres. However, there were definitely areas of wetlands, and this would reduce the amount of land available for development.

As they were getting back in Ron's car, the widow came back out and asked about which lawyer Dave was using. He explained that they hadn't retained an attorney at this time. She strongly suggested against using any of the large Providence law firms, but rather engage one of the local practitioners. Their transactions would go more smoothly and far less expensively. Plus, it would be easier to get the necessary local approvals with one of them representing the developer at the Planning and Zoning Board meetings.

Driving back Ron and Dave laughed at this throwback countrywoman but were both impressed with her smarts. Ron said, "Dave, whatever you do, don't take her threats lightly. Down here, the locals are the law." He also mentioned that he liked the land, and it would be an excellent location for the development, with its wooded areas and panoramic views from the highest points. Dave felt the same way but was nagged by what appeared to be areas of wetlands.

Ron assured him that by his own estimate, there was less than 10% marshland. And he commented, you can always put foot bridges over the wetlands area, and that would only add to the charm of the property."

That night, Dave emailed photos and descriptions of the land to Leo. He suggested that if they liked the parcels, he could have the realtor hire an environmental biology firm to aerial survey the land to determine the extent of the wetlands. He explained that the biologist would determine which areas would be restricted from development. When Leo agreed to spend the $2,500 to get a report on the site, Dave thought about the accomplishments he made in one week. *These are baby steps, but this project is starting to take shape. I better bring Elisa up to date, as she still thinks this is a fantasy.*

Chapter 58

The Offsite Meeting

Over the next few weeks, Dave's staff and the team at the agency worked diligently to complete Project Insight. A couple of writers had been conducting interviews with Brown University professors, hospital administrators, doctors, legislators, and others with interest in the program.

When the written draft was nearly complete, Dave met with Bruce to talk about the introduction announcement.

At about the same time, Dick was getting anxious about releasing the report. He felt they were losing momentum because so much time had passed since the press conference. He called Lyons and told him to schedule an offsite meeting to get an update on the report and preview the announcement program. He suggested having the meeting at one of the hotels in Newport, but he insisted that it start at 11 am.

Of course, Phil Lyons had no idea what to do, so he called Dave and told him to organize it. When Dave told Kathy Cormier to book the event at one of the hotels and include lunch for the expected dozen or so attendees, she said that she would move ahead, but wanted a guest list. Dave told her to get all the names from Lyons for his staff and Dick's invitees. He then called the agency and requested that Bruce, his copy editor, creative chief, and press relations director all attend.

That afternoon, Kathy called back and told him the attendance was now approaching 40, as Dick was bringing his Quad-C group of eight consultants to Newport Country Club to play an early round of golf, and all of them would attend the conference at 11 He also invited several members of Senior Staff.

Chapter 59

The Ambush

On the day of the event, Dave got to Newport early and went over the entire schedule with Kathy including seating, presentation material, and the sequence of speakers. He had Dick scheduled to address the group at the end to close out the nearly all-day meeting.

At 11 o'clock, Dave was prepared to open the meeting, but Dick and his entourage hadn't arrived yet. Kathy got a call from Dick's secretary telling her that they would be about a half hour late. Hearing that, she pushed back the lunch break until one o'clock.

Dave then opened the meeting, explained the delay in the presentation, and filled in the time by giving everyone a background on the steps leading up to the day's presentation. As he completed this warm-up, Dick and his cronies arrived, so Dave moved right into his presentation, using the PowerPoint slides that had been prepared.

It was an imposing display of data and the introduction of *Project Insight*. The presentation included the extensive plan to introduce the project to the people of Rhode Island.

When Dave finished his presentation, he received a round of applause in recognition of the impressive exhibit. But before he could move on, Dick interrupted him and turned to Bruce, saying, "Your agency did a commendable job of putting together this remarkable program. And it is sure to make the impact I was looking for."

Although upset by Dick's slight, Dave started to continue the program when Dick again interrupted him.

"Before we go any further, I have an exciting announcement to make. I have just hired a new executive to join our Senior Management Team. Edgar Davenport will be joining us for lunch. And you can welcome him as RIHIP's new Chief Communications Officer. Now we will have a first-class corporate communications department."

Everyone sat there stunned by this unexpected development.

Dick continued, "Now let's break for lunch. I'm starved."

Kathy ran into the kitchen to tell the manager they were ready for lunch earlier than expected and had one more guest.

As the attendees began to recover from the out of place announcement, they rose and went into the dining room for lunch. Dave looked over to Bruce, but he avoided eye contact, getting up abruptly and leaving the table.

As everyone filed out of the conference room, Dave sat there stunned. Apparently, no one fully realized the significance of Dick's announcement. He was about to be replaced by some outside executive recruited by Dick, and without even discussing it with him. And he was going to introduce him at Dave's off-site

160

conference! For ten minutes he remained in his chair, seething at what had just happened to him.

Chapter 60

AWOL

When he recovered from the shock of this demoralizing development, Dave packed up his briefcase, and without telling anyone, skipped lunch and walked out to the parking lot. There was no way he was going to run the afternoon session of the program. And he was not going to sit there watching Dick introduce his replacement. *Let him have his new executive run the rest of the meeting.*

Driving off the island, he tried to decide where to go. His first thought was to go back to the office, but he quickly rejected that idea. As he came off the bridge in Jamestown, he exited the highway, and drove out to Beavertail Park at the tip of the island.

Dave sat on the rocks, looking out over the Atlantic Ocean, and watching the thundering surf continuously kick waves twenty feet in the air. Over the next couple of hours, he analyzed his situation.

Dick wants me out. That much is obvious. Instead of acknowledging my outstanding effort on this ambitious project, he praised Bruce for the work. And then he hits me with a sledgehammer. He's already hired my replacement and given him my title. I guess I've been fired.

Since he still had six years before he was fully vested in his 401K plan and his retirement benefits, he would have to negotiate an exit package that would make him eligible for the full amount of his benefits.

Beyond that, he had to decide what his next career move should be. He thought about seeking a position with another health insurance company, the golf community project, or moving back into the virtual agency that Elisa was running part-time from their apartment in East Greenwich, RI. While the development project had the most appeal, it was also the longest shot of becoming reality. It could also take a year or two to be launched.

He rejected the option of a job search of other insurance companies despite the reputation he had garnered in the field. He was certain he could land a high paying position at a bigger firm. However, he knew he would never accept an offer from a large bureaucracy and gamble on a similar political situation with its corporate management.

If the golf club project fell through, he and Elisa would rebuild their marketing agency, possibly moving it back to New Jersey. Feeling better now that he had a plan of action, he went home early and told her about his eventful day, and about his next steps. Elisa was angry at Dick for the way he was treating Dave, but she agreed that his plan was the right way to go.

Chapter 61

No Deal

Charles Latham, VP Human Resources had his secretary call Dave and confirm the appointment that Dave had requested. Charlie and Dave had become good friends from the time he arrived at RIHIP, and they continued to enjoy playing golf about once a month.

Charlie was aware of the situation with the new CCO coming in as Dave's boss. It was his job to personally process any candidate for executive status. He had gone to Dick and told him when and how to handle the announcement, and to schedule a one-on-one meeting with Dave before the announcement. Not one to take advice from anyone, he ignored Charlie's recommendations. And this created a dicey situation for HR. With Dick's clumsy handling of the staff change, Dave's remarkable performance history, and bringing in someone who was 20 years younger than Dave as his replacement, this had lawsuit written all over it.

Dave explained the timing of the change, and how it would affect his vesting if he were to leave now. "This move is unwarranted and unprofessional. I'm requesting an exit package that includes my full benefits, plus severance compensation for being forced out early. I relocated here at my personal cost and I'm not going to accept being kicked to the curb."

Charlie thought Dave's requested package was reasonable under the circumstances and agreed to write it up and get Dick to approve it. He was also relieved that Dave was not inclined to be litigious under these circumstances. And he said he would share that posture with Dick. Charlie was certain that if Dave decided to sue RIHIP he would win a big six-figure award. But he was ethically bound not to share that thought with Dave.

The following day, Charlie appeared in Dave's doorway. He looked troubled.

He closed the door and sat down. "Dick has completely rejected the package I showed him. He said that he does not want you to leave, because you are productive and doing a very good job. But if you wish to leave, it's your decision, and there will be no exit package. And of course, if you leave voluntarily, there would be no cause for a lawsuit."

"All of a sudden, Dick thinks I'm productive and doing a good job?"

"Dave, personally, I don't agree with Dick's handling of this situation, or his decision to let you depart without any compensation. But my hands are tied. You have to think about what your next steps should be. If you opt to quit now, you'll be leaving a lot of money on the table. Please think carefully about that. My advice as a friend is to stay with the firm until you are partially or fully invested." With that advice, Charlie made a quick exit.

Dave sat there, seething. He knew Dick had him in an impossible position and was leveraging it to punish him for his successful performance. It was bad enough that Dick had reneged on Al Conover's pledge to make Dave a vice president with its accompanying salary and benefits increase. But between the vesting shortfall and the pension differential over the span of his retirement, Dave would be leaving hundreds of thousands of dollars on the table.

This vindictive bastard is putting me in an impossible bind. He's forcing me to stay in a toxic environment that has become painful to work in. My dream job is a complete disaster

Chapter 62

Sidelined

Bruce called Dave and asked him to come by the agency to discuss details of the Project Insight launch. When he arrived, Dave sensed that Bruce was uncomfortable, but he refrained from asking him about it. Bruce explained that Dick had called him and told him that the agency was to handle the launch and that Dick was going to supervise the entire event himself, and that Dave was not to be involved. He didn't want another fiasco like the press conference. And he also wanted Edgar copied on everything.

Dave was disappointed, but not surprised, particularly with the point of blaming Dave for Dick's poor showing. He said, "I'll have my staff do a final edit of the report, and then get the binders ordered.

"You schedule Dick for the recording of the TV announcement. I'll be glad not to have to go through that again. And you should also write an all-employee memo for Dick to send out. I will tell Kathy Cormier that you will call her with the date for the pre-announcement breakfast. She will set up the event and invite all the people that participated in developing the report. And that should cover it."

"That's great Dave. You're really handling this shit storm like a professional. I admire you for your fortitude."

"Thanks, Bruce. One more question before I leave. You did know about the CCO appointment before the offsite meeting, didn't you?"

"Yes. Dick called me and asked my advice about his choice for the job. He also demanded my confidentiality until the announcement. However, I never thought he would pull a stunt like that at the offsite."

"It just shows his true colors."

"Dave, please understand. RIHIP is one of our largest, most visible clients. I have to protect that relationship. With that said, I would never do anything to hurt you. You have been a friend to me and have always given me the benefit of the doubt in any situation we encountered. And that includes when there was talk of changing agencies. I won't ever forget that."

"Bruce, I fully understand why you had no choice in the situation. I would have handled it exactly the same way you did. After all, I had my own full-size agency for years, so I know what it's like on your side of the desk."

Chapter 63

Tainted Proposal

Edgar Davenport stood timidly outside Dave's office waiting for an invitation to enter. Dave was finishing up a phone call but waved him in and pointed to a seat in front of his desk. He guessed that this was Davenport's first excursion out of his office in the Executive Building. And he was acting as timid as Phil Lyons. *Maybe that's what Dick found attractive about him . . . another lemming.*

Dave had been introduced to Edgar at the last Senior Staff meeting by Phil Lyons, who made one of his rare appearances. With both men having the same title, the introduction felt awkward. Davenport seemed taller than his 5-foot six-inch height because he stood erect, trying to compensate for his height by stretching upward. He was rail thin with a narrow face and a large beak-like nose. His suit was a size too small, which only exaggerated his slight frame. And his skinny tie added an exclamation point to the look. But Edgar added another dimension to his presence with his high-pitched, squeaky voice. Dave noted that physically,

Edgar was exactly the look Dick would find acceptable for Dave's replacement.

As Edgar sat there, he looked around the office and was surprised that it was easily double the size of his cramped space. When Dave got off the phone, Edgar handed him a proposal from State Senator Ken Tedesco. Dave knew Tedesco from a few meetings and RIHIP events that he attended. He had also arranged for Dave to be a guest on one of Tedesco's current-events TV shows. The contents of this proposal called for RIHIP to sponsor a weekly health care TV show that the senator would host on one of the cable access channels.

Edgar explained that Dick wanted Dave to evaluate the show and make a recommendation whether the company should participate in this venture. Dave saw the proposal as an opportunity to help fund Tedesco's run for governor using a seemingly legitimate means to provide TV face time for him. He therefore concluded that funding this show was an ethical breach. Edgar agreed and said that Dick wanted an unbiased opinion from Dave. If he had reservations, Dick would turn down the request.

When Edgar left, Dave wondered why Dick didn't have Edgar prepare the evaluation. But he quickly answered his own question, recognizing that Edgar was a typical corporate minion, lacking any real skills.

Since the project had no redeeming value, Dave wrote a strong memo to reject it. He mentioned the ethical breach, Tedesco's lack of stage presence on his own show, and budget issues, among several other reasons to decline participation and delivered it to Davenport. Edgar scanned the document and said, "Perfect. This is exactly what Dick is looking for. I'll get it to him."

The next morning Edgar called Dave and told him to be at Senator Tedesco's office at 11 o'clock that morning to sign the contract for the TV show. Dick had decided to move forward, despite Dave's recommendation to pass on the offer. And Dick also ordered Dave to delete all copies of his memo from his computer.

Chapter 64

Getting Bogged Down

The FedEx package arrived at the Powers residence in the late afternoon. Seeing that it was from the environmental biology firm that Dave had hired to survey the golf course land, Elisa texted him to let him know that it had arrived.

He got home early, anxious to read the report and see what the wetlands challenges were. The text of the report ran on for pages of technical description of plant life, soil composition, water features, insect and wildlife habitat, etc., none of which meant anything to Dave. As he studied the accompanying topographical maps, he realized that the entire tract contained substantial wetlands, far more than anticipated.

Dave called the office of the environmental firm, and since it was after hours, left a voicemail for a call back to discuss the report. Early the next morning, the chief biologist called him on his cell. He explained that the aerial photography revealed many more areas of wetlands foliage than they saw during their casual walk-through. And from his experience, he suggested to Dave that if he were going to move forward with this project, that he must engage a politically connected consulting firm. He mentioned that the percentage of wetlands would raise a flag, bringing extensive scrutiny to the project. He also commented that, with a qualified architect, the property could be laid out to incorporate the marshes and bogs as design features within the overall design. Dave commented, "Incorporating the wetlands as a design feature would add substantial cost and would require much more land to be purchased to accommodate the project." The biologist agreed.

Following the conversation with the biologist, Dave called Jack Landrieu, told him about the report, and asked him if he could recommend an environmental consultant. Jack suggested, "Great. Let's get together for drinks after work, and I'll take a look at the maps and the report."

At 5:30 they met at Hemenway's where they sat at a table and ordered drinks. Jack began to go over the maps and saw all the areas of gray marking the wetlands designations. He turned to Dave and said, "Look, like so many properties in Rhode Island, this contains a large percentage of restricted acreage. I'm one of the few people in the state that can get approval for your project. As I mentioned, I got the director his appointment to the DEM."

"I can see that, but is it doable?"

"Yes. Let me explain. I am also a consultant to an engineering firm that you will need to hire to do the site plan. It will be expensive, and as you can understand, some of the money you will pay me will be off the books. But make no mistake. If you want to move forward, I'm the one you need to get it done."

After throwing out some large five and six figure budget estimates, Dave told Jack that he would discuss it with his associates and get back to him.

Dave drove home disillusioned and discouraged. This was a huge setback. He was hitting roadblocks with all his plans and career options. Up until he got the report and met with Landrieu, Dave was focused on this undertaking as his next entrepreneurial move to save his sanity.

Now, he thought, *I know I can't go forward with this project if I have to bribe a government official. I promised myself when I was eleven, I would never do anything illegal. And this is as bad as it gets.*

When he got home, he kissed his wife and said, "Lise, we need a vacation. I have to get out of here and recharge my batteries. I'm going to call Joan and ask her if we can use her condo in Florida for a few days."

"David, I love that idea. I've never seen you looking this stressed. You need a break. I'll call Joan tonight and ask her myself. Let's go next week. Can you get away?"

"Lise, I can go anytime. Bruce is handling the Project Insight introduction, and I've got weeks of unused vacation time accruing. Besides Dick will feel better if I'm not around."

Chapter 65

Tickets, Please

Dick had a memo sent to Edgar, regarding the complimentary tickets that Dave distributed to the sales department. He decided that going forward, all tickets should be given to him, as CEO to distribute as he sees fit. Edgar immediately called Dave to his office to discuss the directive.

When Dave arrived, he explained, "Many of our advertising and sponsorship packages include blocks of tickets for given events. For example, our advertising contract with the Providence Bruins includes four tickets for every home game. In addition, the media often sends me tickets from their contracts with the entertainment venues. I give them all to the sales department, and occasionally to my own staff when no none takes them. It's good for morale."

"I am aware of your ticket distribution process, and I already explained it to Dick. He was unconvinced. He claims that he sees you at golf outings, dinners, and other events, and he objects to your participation in those events with the company's vendors."

Angry now, Dave responded, "That insinuation has me fuming. I see Dick at many events because the same companies that invite him often invite me. It is important that I maintain relationships with these contacts through the myriad social events. When Al Conover ran this company, he insisted that I treat our vendors wherever possible. He wanted to be sure there would be no obligation if a vendor bought me lunch or a round of golf. I even have an expense account to cover this entertainment cost."

"I'm aware of all that."

"Yes, you and I have discussed this, and we agree on how I handle it. I know you trust my integrity. Dick, on the other hand, seems to think otherwise. Set him straight because I am outraged."

Dave was still fuming when he walked back to his office.

I can't wait to get out of town for a few days. Elisa and I will use some of the time to figure out our best move forward. I can't put up with this bullshit much longer.

And then he started to again think about the golf course project. *This is the only viable option I have. Maybe if I introduce Leo to Landrieu and have him take care of the bribe, then I can go forward with the development without really knowing about any payoff. Right now, it's the only way I can get out of this shithole.*

Chapter 66

Welcome to Paradise

Almost every year, Siesta Key Beach is named the country's number one beach, and rightfully so. The sand, composed of a quartz mixture is like talcum powder and remains cool to the touch, even on the hottest day at high noon. Dave and Elisa were walking along the edge of the gentle surf at seven in the morning. They had arrived late the day before and were looking forward to a relaxing few days of sun, sand, and golf.

It was a breezy May morning, and with the snowbirds having returned home, they had the beach to themselves. They walked all the way to Point of Rocks and back to the pavilion where their rental car was parked. After breakfast in Siesta Village, they returned to the condo, showered and booked golf for an afternoon round.

That evening, instead of going out to dinner, they ordered take out entrees at one of the nearby restaurants, picked up a bottle of wine, and enjoyed a wonderful evening on the small dock owned by the condo HOA. After eating, they continued to sip the remainder of the wine and watched the sunset over the gulf. Elisa commented, "I love Siesta Key, and all of Sarasota, for that matter. It is so different from the rest of Florida, and a world apart from the Northeast. I definitely could live here."

The next morning over breakfast, they discussed Dave's situation at RIHIP. After sharing some of the details that he hadn't told her about previously, he talked about their options. "I have no choice but to continue at RIHIP for another year until I'm vested in my 401K and pension. However, that's the first stage of the vesting. If I leave then, I get a partial pension when I reach retirement, and I'll get the value of my 401K in the full amount I invested, and only a partial amount the company matched. If I stay, each year those amounts would all increase until I reach full vesting in another five years. But that will never happen. I could never stay that long unless Dick gets hit by a bus."

Seeing the idea forming in her mind, he added, "Don't even think about buying a bus."

"No, but I have my eye on a bulldozer. Among my options, I've already ruled out taking a job with another large insurer. I could never go through this bureaucratic nightmare again. And up until last week, I was seriously considering the golf course development. But now I'm going to have to reject that plan."

Elisa, interrupted, "But why? I was beginning to get excited about the idea of living on a golf course near the beach and us running the operation."

"The wetlands report has thrown the entire project in serious doubt. The only way we're going to get approval is by bribing Jack Landrieu. Leo would be the one handling that, but I still would not be comfortable with it."

178

"David, no. You cannot get even remotely involved with a bribery scheme. Tell me you would never take that risk."

"I considered ways of doing it, but I can't. I have already ruled it out. So that leaves Powers & Others, Inc."

"But I've done very little business in Rhode Island, despite the few referrals you've been able to pass on to me. How can we support ourselves in this environment? It's just not a business-friendly state."

"I kind of agree with you. We can also go back to New Jersey. We were very successful there."

After breakfast, they picked up the local paper and walked back to the condo. Dave started looking for another golf course to play, while Elisa read the news. About 10 minutes into the paper, Elisa commented, "David, look at this. You can buy a brand-new house on a golf course here in Sarasota for under $200,000. How can that be? We should go take a look and see what they are offering."

"I can't imagine it could be anything substantial. But tell you what. Let's see if we can book a tee time at that golf course, and while we're there, we'll look at the models."

The next day after the round of golf, they visited the models. The homes offered in that price range were too small for their needs, but they liked the setting. After rejecting this development, the realtor suggested another golf community that also had modestly priced homes that were larger with three bedrooms.

They got to the models at the second location late in the day and were surprised that the sales office was still open. Walking across the street to the model, they could see clear through the front glass doors and the glass sliders in the back of the house. Their view through the house was the sun setting over the lake in back of the house, and Dave started giggling. Wow! What a spectacular site. "Lise, we're going to buy this house."

"David, you are seriously crazy, but that's why I love you."

On the way back to the condo, they stopped at a casual restaurant for a burger and fries. Elisa brought up the subject of the house they just looked at. "David, you weren't joking about that house, were you?"

"Lise, my love. I am always joking about everything. And I leave it to people to recognize when I'm serious. And you always know without asking. Yes, I am serious. Here's the way I see it. We now have enough money to buy a house in Rhode Island, but there's no way we're staying there."

"Okay, so what do we do?"

"We buy this house. It becomes either our vacation home or our permanent residence depending on our next move. We could certainly consider building a business in this vibrant city."

"I never thought about running a marketing service in a tourist destination."

"I can play golf anywhere in the country and be happy. You love the beach. And this city has the best beach in the world. So why not live here and work here?"

"Well put. When you grow up, you should think about becoming a salesman. I would buy a set of pots from you in a heartbeat."

Chapter 67

Standing on Principle

When they got back home, Dave called Leo and gave him the bad news regarding the wetlands report. As part of the conversation, he told him about his conversation with Jack Landrieu, and his bribery offer. Leo responded, "Dave, what's the big deal? All our investments are in New York City. Greasing the skids there is simply the cost of doing business. We expected that we would have to do the same in a state like Rhode Island. So set it up."

"I'm sorry Leo, I can't be part of that. It's not in my DNA. If you want to move forward, I'll introduce you to Landrieu, but I cannot be an officer of the company. You will have to get someone else to be the project manager. If you'd like, I'll find a qualified builder up here that can run it for you."

"Dave don't be a *cafone*. This deal will make you a millionaire. And you can spend the rest of your life living in a gated community playing golf. How can you pass up a deal like that?"

"Leo, I waited a week to call you about this deal, and I really thought it through. And I looked at every possible angle to come up with a legitimate way to pull it off. It's just not there. The concept is ambitious and exciting. And for me it is extremely tempting. I discussed it with Elisa, and we agreed we just can't do it."

"If that's your final decision, then we're dropping out, as well. You were the catalyst that made the deal attractive. If you change your mind, call me."

Dave's next call was to Bruce. "Can we meet for lunch? I've got something important to discuss with you."

Chapter 68

Greener Pastures

They met at a small Thai restaurant a few blocks from the agency's office and sat at a booth in the back. Although it was near the state capitol, it was not your typical power lunch destination. In fact, they were the only two diners wearing business suits, making it the perfect setting for the conversation Dave needed to have with Bruce.

As soon as they ordered, Bruce led the conversation off, "Before we get into your agenda, I want to take a few minutes to review the final steps of Project Insight, just to make sure we've got it all nailed down." After going over the details, he shared the challenges he had with Dick to prep him for the breakfast address and how useless Edgar was. "Dave, Edgar couldn't make a decision on any issue and had to report back to Dick for approval on every minute detail. It was maddening."

When they were done, Dave said, "Now let me bring you up to date on my situation. As you know, Dick does not want me running the communications department. But at the same time, he wants me to stay with the company. He obviously likes my knowledge and productivity skills, but not anything else about me, particularly my decision-making skills. And this puts me in a quandary."

"Yes, and he needs you to babysit for Edgar because the man can decide if he should pull down his pants to pee."

"Ha! He's leaving me in an impossible position as a company executive, but he won't allow me to exit with a severance package. And he won't accelerate my vesting, should I leave before next year. With that much money on the table, I'm going to stay until I'm at least partially vested. And then we may be moving to Florida. Elisa and I are going to consider restarting our agency in Sarasota and see if we can't get it profitable in a reasonable amount of time."

"Wow. It doesn't take much for you to make a life-changing decision. I can't imagine me making a leap like that. I've been in Rhode Island my entire life. For me that would be inconceivable."

"And for me, so was coming here. And I haven't regretted that move. But now, I'm having some serious reservations."

"Dave, give me a couple of days to digest what you've just told me. My agency has some long-range plans that include Florida. After the Project Insight announcement, I will call to set up another meeting to discuss what I'm thinking."

"Florida? I can't wait to hear what you have in mind."

"But for now, let's have some of the green tea ice cream. It's magical."

Chapter 69

The Big Bang Bust

The final preparations were being completed for the breakfast to announce the Project Insight Report. Thinking about Bruce's experience with Dick, plus his own with Dick in front of a microphone, Dave came up with an idea. He called Bruce and suggested that they do a videotaped announcement instead of a live address to the press during the event, and he told Bruce that behind Dick there should be an assemblage of key consultants that contributed to the report. These would include representatives from Brown University, Rhode Island Medical Society, the Hospital Association, and the legislature.

Bruce thought that it was an excellent recommendation. It would be a great way to acknowledge some of the people who made a huge contribution to the project. And he could have better control over Dick's issues with public speaking.

Unfortunately, when Bruce called Dick to present the idea, he rejected it out of hand. He said, "This is RIHIP's program, and I'm making the announcement alone. I don't need those phonies taking any of the credit for my project. He did quickly agree to do a taped presentation, realizing that it would insulate him from the barrage of questions that were sure to follow.

So, they taped Dick standing in front of the company's boardroom holding the binder containing the few of hundred pages of the report. When the third take was still unacceptable, Dick decided he was done.

The taped announcement at the breakfast was so flat and anti-climactic that it aroused zero interest. The agency then bought a minimal number of commercial spots to air during the evening and nighttime news, expecting the journalists to pick up the story and request interviews with Dick. But that never happened. The outrageously expensive project ended with a whimper, never to be heard from again.

Although the program ran in excess of $1 million, Dick considered it a huge success. At the following Senior Staff meeting he took all the credit, noting, "This blockbuster program stopped the negative legislation in its tracks. Under my direction, the Quad-C team proved to be a formidable force. I've decided to keep it in place to address any other issues that challenge our leadership in the market."

Chapter 70

Unexpected Offer

Back in the same Thai restaurant a week later, Bruce told Dave his plans, and surprised him with a totally unexpected offer. "Dave, as the largest independent ad agency in New England, we've been considering opening an office in Florida. We're thinking about the Orlando area, but we're open to another location, such as Tampa, Jacksonville or Miami. Since you are moving there, I want to engage you to research the various local markets there, make an informed recommendation, and then identify an agency that we can acquire. And if you're interested, I'll consider having you run that satellite office and grow it."

"Wow. That was totally unexpected. I had no idea you were interested in Florida."

"I also have another offer for you to consider. While you are doing your research, and after you move, would you be interested in pitching our agency with some of the health insurance contacts that you've made through the Association. I would be willing to pay you a $100,000 retainer for one year if you consider both tasks. And after the first year, we can negotiate a long-term deal. Is this of any interest to you?"

"Bruce, those are two fascinating ideas. I was thinking along the lines of making sales calls on a few health insurers where I have strong contacts. And I was going to suggest that to you. But the agency search project is coming out of left field. I had no idea you were seriously interested in going 1,000 miles away to open an office."

"Dave, Florida is exploding. And think about the residual benefit. Visits to our Florida office easily become vacation trips. And I'm certainly looking for more leisure time, particularly in a warm climate during the winter."

"Then in that case, you definitely want Sarasota. It is truly *Paradise*. I never thought I would even consider living in Florida, until I began vacationing in that beautiful small city."

"OK. I was sure you would want to do this, so let's shake on the deal. Of course, the decision regarding location will have to be made on more than the best place for a vacation. I have no timetable. You can start whenever you complete your exit from RIHIP. And we'll keep it confidential between us."

"Bruce, I will probably do one more Association conference in the next few months, and I may be able to make some discreet inquiries while I'm there. And I will also be taking at least another trip or two to Florida before I quit. I can do some research during that next stay. But we'll start the clock after I leave the company."

Chapter 71

A Fish Out of Water

Despite the fact that Dave was not stripped of his CCO title, the new Chief Communications Officer, Edgar Davenport was now using the same title. Dave rarely used his, so it was no big deal for him to simply discontinue using it. And after a few interactions with Davenport, his suspicion was confirmed. Edgar was a typical bureaucrat, mindlessly nodding affirmatively regardless of what you were telling him. He was also woefully weak in all aspects of his role as CCO. But that's what Dick wanted, a puppy dog he could train.

Edgar was constantly calling Dave into his office with questions about even the most trivial activity. Production queries were to be expected, but basic communications issues would be the kind of areas a seasoned professional should know from experience. Dave's job description was rapidly evolving from managing the department and coordinating the ad agency activity, to being a wet nurse to Edgar. Unfortunately, Davenport's mind was more like a rock than a sponge, so repetition became a large part of the education process. And Edgar's stuttering only increased during Dave's explanatory lectures.

At this point, the communications department was still in a different building on the campus than the executive suite, so Dave continued to hold his weekly staff meetings without Lyons or Davenport attending. And this proved to be one of the few tasks that Dave still relished about his job.

At the most recent meeting, one of the writers brought in a guest that wanted to pitch an idea for a segment of the TV show. She introduced the woman from a psychiatry research center in Cranston. The guest wanted to discuss her study on mentally triggered illnesses. Donna Marino welcomed the visitor and then asked each staff member to give his or her name and job function. When it was Dave's turn, everyone turned to the guest knowing Dave was going to trigger a reaction with one of his offbeat remarks. And he didn't disappoint. "Hi, my name is David, and I'm a hypochondriac."

Testing New Markets

There was a direct marketing conference coming up in Key West at the end of the month. Fortunately, Dave had processed the request months before Davenport came on board. He waited until two weeks before the event to tell Edgar about it and advised him that it was too late for him to sign up, but he would let him know when the next event was announced.

At the conference, Dave arranged to have dinner with a couple of colleagues from Florida First Health Insurers. Since both states had high percentages of seniors, they had worked together the year prior and co-produced a successful promotion for a Medicare insurance program for seniors.

Dave told the two executives that he was leaving RIHIP and was going to be working for the agency that had produced all the terrific marketing programs for his company. In sharing the news, he also mentioned that he was moving to Florida, and would be calling on them to pitch business for the agency. The response was enthusiastic and encouraging, and this prompted Dave to open dialog with some of the marketing execs from other insurance companies who were at the conference. The VP from New Hampshire said to him, "Dave, everyone admires your work and would love to have access to that level of creativity. When you get settled, come and see me."

Following the conference, instead of returning to Rhode Island, Dave rented a car and drove to Sarasota where he spent a few days. He had scheduled a meeting in advance with the CEO of the local Chamber of Commerce. When they met, he explained that he was consulting for a large New England advertising agency that was looking to acquire a shop in Florida. The plan was to add some staff from Providence and then substantially grow the local agency.

The Chamber's CEO was excited about the prospect and set up meetings with two of the three major agencies in the community. The third agency, which was the largest, had no interest in a merger, acquisition or even meeting with a representative from another firm. This surprised Dave that the owner didn't even want to hear what he had to say.

Dave visited the other two and came away disheartened, as they were both very small, not much larger than graphic design studios. He then expanded his search radius to Tampa and Orlando and still found none of them suitable. In fact, he was extremely disappointed at the level of creativity he uncovered. In Orlando, the few agencies he visited were all tied into Disney and had no interest in a merger opportunity.

Returning to Sarasota, Dave went to the Ringling School of Design, a college with national recognition for the recruitment level of its graduating students. The dean, who was delighted to meet with him, explained that a large percentage of the students majored in animation, and upon graduation left town for either Los Angeles or Orlando, the two cities with the largest concentration of animation studios.

Dave returned to Rhode Island with mixed emotions. He was delighted with the prospects for clients for the agency but saw no opportunity in the greater Sarasota area for an acquisition. And this was quickly ruling out southwest Florida as the location of Bruce's satellite office.

Chapter 74

Follow the Sun

Upon returning to Providence, Dave met with Bruce at his office early one morning. He presented his report, most of which pleased Bruce. He was delighted by the prospect of doing business with Florida First Health Insurers and some of the insurers from other states.

Dave was not interested in relocating in any other city but Sarasota, so if he found an agency elsewhere to be acquired, he would not become its COO. He would take over the operation on an interim basis and then recruit and train his replacement.

Bruce reluctantly accepted this idea but was really anxious to get situated somewhere in Florida. What convinced him to work on Sarasota longer was the copy of one of the city's lifestyle magazines, which Dave gave him. It was probably three times the size of Rhode Island Magazine, a publication that serves four times the population of Sarasota. And making it more impressive was the fact that there were three lifestyle magazines for one small city and each of them carried substantially more advertising pages than Rhode Island's one statewide publication.

Following his meeting with Bruce and discussing his findings, he was more anxious than ever to get moving forward on his next adventure.

Chapter 75

Homecoming?

Elisa was getting ready to leave the apartment to do some shopping when she got a phone call. "Elisa, it's Lucy, your tenant in Ramsey."

"Hi Lucy, how are you? Is everything okay with the house?"

"The house is fine. I could live here forever. But there's a problem." She began crying and couldn't speak.

"Lucy, what wrong? How can I help you? Are the kids okay?"

Still crying, she said, "None of us are okay. My bastard husband is divorcing me. He has taken up with his secretary and wants to marry her."

"Oh, no. That's horrible. How can he leave a beautiful family like yours?"

Between sobs, Lucy continued, "Oh, he's gonna pay. This divorce will cost him plenty. I hope the bimbo is worth it. But I have to move out. We're going back to Long Island to live with my parents. They'll take care of us until this is settled. I hope you understand. I hate leaving this place."

"Lucy don't' worry about it. Take care of the kids. I wish you well."

When she hung up, she called Dave and shared the news with him. And she thought, *I feel bad for her, but I'm happy with being able to move back to our beautiful house. This will certainly affect our future plans*

Chapter 76

Bureaucratic Workload

Over the next couple of months, Dave spent most of his time teaching Edgar how to do his job. But it was futile. He realized that you just can't inject new ideas into a rock-hard substance.

Edgar never acknowledged Dave's generosity for sharing of his expertise. But he at least treated Dave to lunch at least once a week. And one day at lunch, he made a welcome suggestion to Dave. "Since you come in so early in the morning, why not take advantage of the flex schedule, and leave early? You don't have to put in 10 or 12 hours a day."

Dave had never considered that option but decided to start doing it. "You're right. With two of us sharing the load, I'll put in a standard day, regardless of the time I arrive."

He usually came in between six and seven in the morning, so on select days when he wanted to play golf, he would come in at six, work through lunch, and leave at one. He would then eat a sandwich on the way to the course and be playing by two. Once a week or so,

198

Elisa would join him. And occasionally Bruce would take the afternoon off and play a round with him.

On the days that he didn't play, he would work from home and research prospects that he planned to call on once he left the company.

Chapter 77

More Bags

Denise Moran sat in Dave's office going over the myriad of brochures, and other promotional material that was in the pipeline for completion. During the meeting she commented that the requests for reorders of the pharmacy bags from Landrieu's company has been increasing, both in quantity and frequency. Dave responded, "My guess is that the pharmacists are hoarding the bags, expecting that we will discontinue the program, so they are trying to make this perk last as long as possible. It's such an inexpensive promotion, given the cost per impression, that I wouldn't give it a second thought. And besides, it's the only effort we make to improve our relations with these independent pharmacies. And besides, besides, it's Phil's problem. He's in control of the program, and I'm not allowed to contact Jack Landrieu."

Denise commented, "Are you kidding? You mean, I'm allowed to talk to Landrieu and you're not? Isn't that a hoot!

"A bureaucracy is a wonderful thing to behold. Don't you think?"

Laughing, she continued, "As far as the bag orders go, this is one of the easiest production projects I handle. With the vendor handling the warehousing and distribution, I have very little to do. There is no tying in all the paperwork that Purchasing requires. The cost per thousand has only changed slightly.

"I wish our other printing orders could be processed this simply. It sometimes consists of 20 pages of documentation."

"Yes, the process is an organizational nightmare, but we do get to control the vendor selection. And that's what we fought so hard for."

"I still can't believe you pulled that off. In a big corporation, it's easier to levitate than to get some self-important middle manager to give up even the most trivial task within his area of responsibility."

"It wasn't that difficult. These career executives have never faced anyone with imagination. And that's what scares Nichols and his band of merry men."

"You mean Quad-C? How can the conference room contain that much hot air?"

Chapter 78

Inspirational Sales Management

At the monthly Sales Department meeting, the AVP, Jeff Ryan reported that sales had been leveling off for some time, and more recently actually began to drop. Ryan did his usual pep talk, right out of the sales manual, and encouraged his team to step up their effort. One of the reps raised his hand and said that the brokers were reporting a slowdown in leads generated, and this could be affecting the overall volume of new business.

To that, Ryan countered, "You people are supposed to be professionals. Go out and find your own leads. I expect results, not excuses." And with that he closed the meeting.

That directive was typical of Ryan. His office was filled with sales manuals and motivational books. And he quoted from all of them. Added to that persona, he had a General Patton complex, and loved to shout orders to his sales reps. Dave kept expecting him to start carrying a riding crop.

Joan, who made one of her infrequent visits to the sales meeting, came up to Dave and asked him to accompany her back to her office. When they sat at her small conference table, she asked about the complaint regarding the lead generation.

Dave responded, "We're doing far less advertising now, and what we're doing is so pedestrian that it's not registering with the viewers. The frequency of the message is only part of the formula. The message itself has to connect with the audience. The drivel that Dick insists on running is just wasting money. And the market response is telling you exactly that."

"Well, I'm going to show him the sales reports and demand that we get back to doing the type of advertising that you have always produced. My bonus relies on growing the sales numbers."

Joan don't waste your time. I'll be gone in a couple of months, and Davenport will never produce the kind of communications programs that are needed. It's not in his DNA. And Dick won't allow anything creative. It's beyond his comprehension."

"And speaking of your departure, I want to have a small sendoff party for you before you leave. We'll just invite the sales and marketing staff, and we'll hold it in the cafeteria."

"Joan, that's not necessary. I was just planning to have a lunch or cocktail party for my team in Communications."

"Dave, I know both the Sales Department and Product Marketing want to be part of any event we have. So let me organize it. I promise I will keep it small. And you can still take your team out to lunch, as well."

Chapter 79

Welcome Home

When Elisa returned from her trip to Sarasota and landed at Green Airport, she walked through the gate area to the exit. Standing outside the restricted area were several limo drivers waiting for passengers. They were all holding signs with the names of the passengers they were picking up. In their midst stood Dave, wearing a dark suit, black tie, sunglasses, and a chauffer's cap holding a sign that read, "POWERS".

Playing along, she said, "Excuse me sir. You're not the driver I requested."

To which Dave answered, "Well pardon me. I was told to pick up a fat, dumpy broad that looks like she got run over by a truck. That can't possibly be you, as I don't see any trucks. Can I see some identification?"

"OK smartass, take my bag and get me home."

As they walked down the hall and into the apartment, Elisa was hit by a magnificent aroma. "What did you make me for dinner? I can't believe how good it smells in here."

"Since it's Friday, this is an alternative to our date night."

On the stove was a huge pot of bouillabaisse and on the counter a fresh loaf of crusty Italian bread. The Mediterranean stew filled the air with the aroma of lobster, shrimp, mussels, scallops, and cod. Elisa looked at the perfectly set table and the spotless kitchen. "This is nothing short of a minor miracle. I guess I'm too used to seeing your kitchen disasters."

Dave smiled, "When I cook, I don't work neat. I work fast. It's all about the timing. You know that by now."

She checked out the laundry room, which had no dirty clothes. And the bed was made.

With the dinner simmering, and the bread in the oven, Dave poured the wine. Elisa lifted her glass in a toast and said, "If you weren't already married, you would probably make a beautiful wife for someone."

Chapter 80

New Business

Although Dave always got up before Elisa in the morning, on this Saturday, he found her in the kitchen preparing breakfast. As he poured coffee, she said, "I thought I'd reciprocate for your wonderful dinner last night." That's when he noticed the huge omelet she was preparing.

She served the meal on the balcony and when they were nearly done, she said, "I didn't want to spoil your surprise dinner last night, but I have a serious issue to discuss with you."

Always unflappable, he asked, "Are you divorcing me? You found a sugar daddy down there, didn't you? Can he cook?"

"No such luck, even though I walked around in a bikini. In between shopping, I did do some cold calling to get a feel for the market down there. And I'm very concerned. Other than hospitality, there is no industry in Sarasota. And the business climate is not at all attractive."

"You determined this in one week, while shopping for furniture?"

"I called on some hotels. The chain properties, like Hilton, all use the agency for the parent company. The local motels do not advertise. All the independent businesses are reluctant to use any outside firms that come into the area. I found that shocking."

"Interesting you say that. I got a similar response when I called on the agencies on behalf of Bruce's company. They just don't want to talk to strangers."

"As that was all sinking in, I began to panic. But I got a call from my friend, DeeDee. Her uncle fired their ad agency, and she wants to meet me so I can advise her on what to do. They have a multi-million-dollar budget, and she would love for us to handle it."

Dave's wheels are already turning, and Elisa sees that he's on the same page as her. She said, "What seems like a logistical monster is actually an opportunity. Our tenant in Ramsey has been out of the house for two months. We could move back anytime."

Extending her thought, Dave said, "So we move back to Ramsey, take on Dizzy Don's and fire up our agency again there. What about Sarasota?"

"We're not selling that house. Then I *would* divorce you. We'll become snowbirds, like everyone else. I think there's some business potential there, but it will take a few years to develop. And there's the potential projects from First Florida that you can handle for Bruce."

Chapter 81

Quid Pro Quo

Dave looked up to see Denise standing in his doorway. "Why are you standing there? Come on in."

"You were concentrating on your laptop screen so intensely that I didn't want to break your chain of thought."

"Well now that I've lost my place in this comic book I'm reading online, tell me what's so important?"

"I love the way you make a joke of everything. No matter how dire the situation, we can always depend on you to lighten the atmosphere.

"And this issue is not that important. I just got request from Steve Fisher to place another order for prescription bags. And this time it includes a 10% price increase. But what surprised me was that the email was forwarded by Phil Lyons instead of coming directly to me."

"You interrupted my comic book reading to tell me that? Big deal. Lyons is most certainly trying to use these orders to elicit some favors from Jack Landrieu. So, he probably told Landrieu to send all the requests through him. If you recall, Lyons initiated the project when he made the introduction to Landrieu a few years ago. And as I mentioned recently, he told me not to have any contact with Landrieu. Going back to the beginning I assumed this was a legitimate political quid pro quo, similar to the way business is done in this state. But now I see it differently."

"Dave, as an outsider, you certainly didn't take long to figure out the Rhode Island model that dominates how business is conducted. There's a string attached to everything."

Chapter 82

Consulting Gig

Edgar Davenport called Dave to his office for an update meeting. He and Dave sat and reviewed the existing projects, all of which were flowing normally. Edgar then asked about the TV show, and Dave explained that the next one-hour special was in the early stages of planning. Most of the actual segment topics had not been decided yet.

Davenport then mentioned that Dick was getting tired of the current advertising campaign and wanted Edgar to develop a new series of ads. But this time, he wanted more excitement.

Dave laughed and said, "I guess Joan threatened him. Take Dick out of the commercials, and that in itself would be a marked improvement."

Edgar smiled, and said, "I told Dick that you should develop and direct the campaign with the agency. But he wants me to do it, although he reluctantly agreed that you probably should participate in the process."

"Edgar, I'm leaving in a few weeks. I could help develop the concept, but I'll be gone long before any production takes place."

"Well, that's why I really wanted to sit and talk to you. I'll be the first to admit that I don't have your creative or production skills. I want to offer you a consulting contract to continue to work with me on these complex projects. Would you consider it?"

"I would certainly consider a consulting gig. That's how I started here. And it's the only way I would ever be able to work for the company with some autonomy. What do you have in mind?"

"I'd like to offer you three days a week, twice a month in Providence and ancillary time, as needed working from home. Your fee will be $15,000 per month, plus expenses of course. We'll start with six months and continue from there. I can sign off on six-month increments without any other approvals. We'll keep your email account active, and I'll set you up with a small office to use when you're here."

They shook hands on the deal, and Dave floated back to his office. *I can't believe the opportunity that was just presented to me. I could continue to direct the TV show and produce a new ad campaign. These are my two favorite projects and getting well paid for these enviable assignments. The potential of $180,000 a year is far better than the severance deal I fought for and lost last year.*

As he thought about the fee from Bruce, plus some other projects on the horizon, he did the calculation. *I will be making about double what I was paid when I came to RIHIP as a consultant. And it would be on my terms without the stress of Dick Nichols second-guessing me at every turn.*

Chapter 83

Adios Amigos

The cafeteria in the headquarters building at RIHIP was on the lower level and easily accommodated over 200 people for a sit-down meal. By removing the tables, it can be set up auditorium style to seat over twice that number. It also had a moveable dais that could be arranged along the front wall. When not used for dining, it frequently served as a meeting facility for large groups of staff members, outside visitors, and other guests.

The farewell tribute was scheduled for four-thirty, but people began arriving as early as four. When Dave arrived at about 4:20, there wasn't an empty seat, and about 100 people were standing in the back. Looking around, Dave thought, *So much for my request to limit the size of my small farewell sendoff.*

Joan, glowing and waving to people in the crowd was standing up front and beckoned Dave over. He said to her, "I suppose all this was your doing."

"Dave, I tried to accommodate your wishes, but people have been calling me all day asking if it was okay for them to come. And as you can see, employees from every department are here. But don't expect Dick or Phil Lyons to attend. I saw them leave for *lunch*, but they were dressed to play golf."

At a little past 4:30 Joan welcomed the crowd of several hundred that was now overflowing into the hallways. She began to cite all of Dave's accomplishments in his five years with the company and said that RIHIP's turnaround success would not have been achieved without Dave's brilliant branding, marketing, and communications programs.

Joan was a marvelous speaker, and the crowd was getting raucous. She then introduced Dave to thunderous cheers.

"Wow! Thank you everyone. I am truly overwhelmed by the huge crowd that has gathered here today. I would never have believed so many people would take time after hours just to get a free donut and a soft drink." And turning to Joan, asked, "Is all this coming out of my expense account?"

The laughter gave him a chance to stop for a moment, as he began to choke up. He was a competent speaker who always relished the opportunity to address a crowd. Holding back tears, he continued, "I can't understand why I'm becoming so emotional lately. Elisa says it must be my medication. But I never thought cholesterol meds could cause this kind of side effect. Maybe it's the legal marinara I'm putting on my pasta."

As his audience burst out laughing uproariously, he looked around the assemblage, recognizing that every Senior Staff member was in attendance, along with their administrative teams, including Dick and Phil's secretaries. Also present were the entire sales and marketing departments.

Dave became overwhelmed by this outpouring of support and recognition. And he continually had to stop to hold back the tears. With all his public speaking, he'd never experienced anything like it before.

He closed by saying, "During my tenure here I have achieved the height of my success. And that exciting milestone was possible only because of my incredibly creative team. Every one of them contributed their ideas and recommendations to the process. Please honor them with a round of applause."

Everyone seated stood up and clapped for several minutes as Dave barely contained his emotions. He closed by saying he would always remember the wonderful experience the job brought him, as well as the many people that he was so fortunate to work with. The standing ovation was so loud he thought the acoustical tiles would start falling from ceiling.

Chapter 85

Taking Care of Business

Arriving back in Ramsey, Dave hit the ground running. He and Elisa had an appointment to meet with DeeDee and following that, they were both going to meet with her uncle, Don. Elisa had been working on some new ad ideas for the Dizzy Don's appliance chain while they were still in Rhode Island. And she presented them to DeeDee. Not expecting any creative submissions, she was ecstatic. She said, "Don will love these."

They discussed the terms of their working relationship and after agreeing to all the details, they went in and sat with Don. Elisa greeted him in Italian, "Buongiorno, signore Don."

Noticeably pleased, he got up and kissed her on both cheeks. He then explained that he was delighted to have them handle the account, and DeeDee would be making all the decisions.

The following week, Dave drove to Providence and spent most of the three days at the agency with Edgar by his side. At home, Elisa began preparing ads for the next newspaper campaign. Dave flew from Providence to Sarasota to make some calls in that area.

He set up appointments with every small and large company he could get in to see, pitching his virtual agency concept. At the end of the week, Dave came up empty handed. Not one company he met with was interested in exploring an opportunity any further. There were many reasons given. Most had concerns that his out-of-town agency did not understand the local market. But as Dave concluded, it was a closed community, and there was a distrust of anyone coming there to launch a business.

Shifting gears, Dave made calls to set up appointments with his colleagues at health insurers around the country. Interestingly and despite all the encouragement he got at the last conference he had attended; he encountered a lot of subtle rejection. This came in the form of delaying any meeting with him for several months and using the excuse of preferences to favor local vendors, rather than bringing in someone from out of state. The most encouraging conversation came from Florida First, so Dave arranged to drive to Jacksonville and meet with the marketing executives there.

At their lunch meeting, he explained that he was working on establishing a satellite branch of the New England agency in Florida, and that he would be running it. In the interim, he could manage any programs and campaigns as account executive and have them implemented in Providence. The Florida First team liked the idea of getting Dave's creativity, backed by a major agency. And they discussed some possible programs. They told Dave that they would look at their upcoming schedule and see where he could get involved. Dave arrived back home, tired, but exhilarated by the positive reception and potential from First Florida.

Chapter 86

The Grim Reaper

After making sales calls in New Jersey for a few days, Dave flew to Providence, arriving late morning. He went directly to RIHIP headquarters to meet with Davenport. Edgar gave him a brief update on activity and was excited to tell him that they were getting ready to start developing a new ad campaign. "When you come up again in two weeks, we'll have a meeting at the agency to discuss the timeframe for the project, but in the meantime, I want you to start coming up with ideas for the concept. I want this to be the best ad program RIHIP has ever developed, so I'm counting on you for your best work."

Before Dave could respond, Dick Nichols walked up to Edgar's office doorway and said to him, "When you get done here, I need to see you about the next airing of the Tedesco TV show."

His mouth dropped when he realized Dave was sitting in the office, but he turned and left without acknowledging him.

Dave smiled at Dick's rudeness but responded to Edgar's statement, "That's great. I've been looking forward to working on the new ads. I'll be putting in some time on the next TV special while I'm here, but I already have some thoughts on a concept for the new campaign."

When Dave got back to Ramsey, he got a strange email from Edgar. The brief content read, "Dave, since there are no projects scheduled for you at this time, I see no need for you to return to RIHIP in two weeks. When any new programs come up that require your assistance, we will request your participation. Edgar"

Shocked, Dave called Edgar immediately, but got his voicemail. Rereading the memo, and thinking about it, he became convinced that this apparent cancelling of his consulting contract had all to do with Dick seeing him in Edgar's office. The following week, he got another email putting his consulting contract on hold.

Chapter 87

Coming Out of the Closet

Elisa was planning their next trip to Sarasota when she got a call from an acquaintance that she had met at a wedding in Newport the year before. The woman, Joanne Sawyer was a partner in a custom closet company that was based in southwest Florida and wanted to explore a possible new ad campaign. Delighted by the outreach, Elisa told her they could meet in two weeks when we got to Sarasota.

After arriving back in Florida, Dave and Elisa drove to Fort Myers and met with Joanne and her two partners.

At the meeting, the CEO showed them their previous ads and commented that they never produced enough business to justify the expense, so they stopped advertising and relied on direct sales calls to builders and homeowners. Reviewing the ads, Dave responded, "These look exactly like the ads of every other closet company. They are just beauty shots of fancy closets, neatly stacked with clothes and shoes. They don't stand out against the competition. If you blocked the names at the bottom, you couldn't tell one from another."

Seeing the confused look on the three partners, Dave explained, "How can you stand out when your ads look like the same as the competition? What if we took these same beautiful closets and put some people in them or created unexpected situations in a closet." Picking up a photo from the table he continued, "For example, picture this closet with a formally dressed couple serving cocktails and canapés. Would that get attention? It would create a buzz and have a direct effect on your sales."

Joanne and the CEO immediately recognized the potential of this unique idea. However, their third partner, a left-brain wonder, who handled fabrication and installation, was convinced that it was a dumb idea and a waste of money. But the decision was made to move ahead. Dave and Elisa began developing the program.

Since establishing their residence in Sarasota several months ago, this was their first major advertising campaign. And it was a huge success. Joanne was able to directly tie several new clients to the reaction from the ads. But more importantly, the editor of the local business publication saw the ads and contacted Dave. He recognized the creativity used in the campaign to build the closet company's brand.

As a result, he interviewed Dave and wrote an article about his branding and marketing philosophy. The brief but flattering article got the attention of the owners of the local agencies who became jealous and annoyed by this implied endorsement by the newspaper. It also further alienated them from Dave and Elisa's fledging company. And it pretty much closed the door on any local opportunity to arrange a merger with Bruce's agency.

The article, however, did get noticed by the CEO of the largest credit union in the greater Sarasota area. He called Dave directly and set up a meeting to see what they could do for his organization.

Chapter 88

Take It to the Bank

The meeting with Thomas Randolph and his marketing VP turned out to be more of a seminar on branding than a sales pitch. They were both fascinated by the concept of building a brand, rather than advertising a rate reduction. Randolph explained that the growth of the credit union was flat. And they were looking to build their customer base beyond the original membership which came from the teacher's union and the local newspaper union. At the end of the meeting, Tom requested a proposal, and commented that he wanted to begin quickly with a program.

Driving back, Elisa was excited by this very visible prospect. She really liked the executives they met and saw their need for a branding and marketing campaign. Thinking about the amount of time that would be needed to service this client, they estimated a reduced hourly rate of $125 rate and proposed a $5,000 per month fee. She suggested that the proposal include a review of time and services at the end of three months. If the hours varied substantially, they could discuss a fee change up or down with the client.

Dave went back to the credit union headquarters the next day and presented their proposal. Tom accepted it on the spot, and appreciated the review clause, commenting that it made the deal eminently fair. Surprised by the immediate acceptance, Dave called Elisa when he left and told her the news. "Lise, we just landed our largest local client. And I think they will be around for a long time. We're going to have to manage our time between New Jersey and Florida."

As soon as they got back to Ramsey, DeeDee gave them a rush newspaper campaign for a small appliance promotion. That got Dave thinking that he would have to spend more time in Sarasota, while Elisa spent more time in New Jersey.

Chapter 89

Shifting Gears

The product manager for Medicare Supplement at Florida First sent Dave an email and invited him to attend a strategy session with him in Jacksonville. The meeting ran over two hours and, as typical with bureaucracies, nothing was accomplished. Dave was able to make a few recommendations, based on programs he had implemented in Rhode Island, and everyone was impressed with his input.

Dave subsequently attended two more meetings over the next few months, but none of the programs ever got off the ground. He called the VP of Advertising and Marketing and discussed the situation with him. "Peter, I keep driving up to Jacksonville, a nine-hour round trip, and coming home empty-handed. Am I wasting my time?"

"Dave there is no way we would continue to bring you in if there wasn't going to be a payoff. Please have patience, as we are particularly slow at launching new campaigns. So don't become discouraged. You will be rewarded, I promise."

About a week later, Dave got a call from Bruce, asking about progress on the prospects Dave was pitching. Dave explained that he was convinced that there were no potential acquisition prospects anywhere from Tampa to Naples. He had made one trip to Orlando, but with so much of the marketing promotion controlled by Disney or tied into them, he didn't see any prospects or opportunities there either.

Bruce asked, "What about the health insurers? Any potential on the horizon?" Dave explained that he had given up on most of the contacts he had around the country, but Florida First had assured him of some business very shortly.

Bruce hesitated a second, and said to Dave, "We're going to have to cancel our arrangement with you and discontinue your fee. It has now been a year, and we have nothing to show for it. I agree that our plan to have a Florida agency may not be viable at this time, so we're going to shelve that idea. Going forward however, if you are able to generate some sales with Florida First, or any other company, we'll compensate you with a full commission.

And Dave, I have no regrets about paying you the $100,000 fee for the past year. And it was a fee not a draw, so you owe us nothing. You have certainly been good to us ever since we began to work together. So hopefully, if you can get us a campaign or two, you can earn a commission, and we can continue our working relationship. I would like nothing better."

Dave hung up and thought, Bruce is a stand-up guy. *He's willing to walk away from 100K and not demand even a partial payback. I'm sure some of that money is a reward for the profitable relationship he had at RIHIP under my watch. He's probably working much harder to make a profit from them now.*

Chapter 90

A New Client

About a month later, Dave got a call from Peter at Florida First. "Dave, I've got a project I want you to work on. It's not the kind of program that I had envisioned for you, but it's really important. In fact, it came down from the CEO himself."

"Peter, I don't care if you want me to lick stamps and mail solicitation letters to seniors, I just want to get a project from you on the books."

"This is going to be a huge research project, that has a dual purpose. You are going to travel the state and interview every independent brokerage that handles our products. You'll then write a report on your findings with recommendations to improve our relationship with these brokers. And if it all works out as I expect, you will get to implement whatever plan you propose.

"We're having serious issues with the brokers, and we're hoping this project will prevent an upheaval in this sales channel. The CEO got a budget estimate from one of the big national consulting firms for $250,000 plus expenses to put a team in Florida and run the research. And they always run well over budget and well beyond schedule. I'd like you to take the project on for about $200,000, as I'd like you to show up the big national consultant. I will provide someone from the sales support team to work and travel with you. If you agree, write up a brief proposal based on this information and email it to me. We want to start in a week."

"That sounds great. I can certainly manage this project, and I can do it within your budget. The timeframe to start is also no problem, and you can expect it will be completed before deadline. I'll get right on it and have the proposal to you this afternoon."

After the call, Dave thought about the project, and considered billing it through Bruce's agency. He decided to run this assignment himself, as it was really a one-man research assignment. If the second half of the assignment came through as expected, that would be a much larger project. It would be better suited for Bruce's agency to run it and bill it directly. The agency would make a hefty profit, and it would offset some of the money they paid Dave without having received anything in return. It would also be good to get his agency's name on the books at Florida First.

After Dave sent in the proposal, he called Bruce and explained the project he was getting from the insurer. He also shared his decision to have the agency implement the second phase when it came through. Bruce was delighted and thanked Dave profusely. Bruce agreed that Dave should run the research effort through his own company and keep Bruce in the loop as the program developed. The much bigger prize would be the second phase, and Bruce was already salivating at getting that huge assignment.

The Deliverables

The project took three months to complete, including the presentation of the report. And during that timeframe, Dave flew back home twice for a week each. While in New Jersey, he made sure he had a face-to-face meeting with each client on their books.

To complete the research project, he traveled around the state with the sales associate, who had in-depth knowledge of all the key brokers. The key takeaway was that the brokers were requesting a marketing campaign to help them build sales in their specific local markets.

There were two key recommendations that came out of the report. The first was that the company partner with health care providers to set up health clinics in the inner cities for the large Hispanic populations were underserved in these areas and had difficulty purchasing insurance.

The second recommendation was to develop a localized marketing plan promoting the broker network in each market within the state. None of the other insurers offered this, and it would set Florida First apart from their competition.

The presentation meeting for the report, which was held at the Jacksonville headquarters. Following the meeting, many of the staff in attendance came up and congratulated Dave on his thorough report. They also felt confident that a budget would be approved for the campaign he recommended. He left the meeting satisfied that the company got a very good value for their expenditure, and he looked forward to getting the assignment to implement the long-term marketing campaign.

Chapter 92

Breaking News

A front page, headline story broke on Sunday in The Rhode Island Observer. It exposed a television show that aired on a public access cable station featuring State Senator Ken Tedesco as host and producer, and it was being solely sponsored by Rhode Island Health Insurance Partners. The investigative journalist that uncovered the story claimed that this was a major ethical violation between the senator and RIHIP. Tedesco headed up the Corporations Committee in the Senate and controlled most of the legislation pertaining to health insurance.

When questioned by the journalist regarding the details of the story, the press spokesperson at RIHIP claimed that the company knew nothing about the show, had no knowledge of sponsoring it, and had nothing to say that would support the allegation. The journalist then called the local cable company and spoke to the president. He confirmed that Tedesco contacted him directly and told him that RIHIP was funding all the costs for the show including production.

Completing her due diligence, the journalist then tracked down Dave Powers in Sarasota, as he and Elisa were spending Thanksgiving week there. Dave was taken by surprise that she located him for comment. He was not surprised at the story itself, as his evaluation of the show had strongly urged the company to reject the proposal on ethics grounds.

Dave told the reporter that he had nothing to say at this time, and he had to discuss the situation with others before being interviewed.

A couple days later, a second story broke. This one, by the same reporter told the story about a lucrative prescription bag contract with the Rhode Island House Speaker, Jacques Landrieu. And once again the reporter called Dave for comment. And again, he blew her off. But now he was concerned. He immediately called Edgar but got his voicemail and left an urgent message. His next call was to Joan, but her secretary told him that she was out of town and would call him back next week. Frustrated, Dave called Bruce, got his voicemail and again, left an urgent message.

The Scapegoat

It was late Friday afternoon, and still no one had returned Dave's calls to Rhode Island. He tried Bruce a second time, and again got his voicemail. He was now getting really upset, as he wanted to talk to the reporter. In her probing questions, there was an inference that he had been conducting operations at RIHIP to funnel money to politicians without approval from top management. He wanted to set the record straight, but he needed to know what the company spokesperson had been telling her.

On Saturday morning, a call came in from Joan. "Thank God you called back."

"Don't *Thank God* me. Do you have any idea of the crisis you've unleashed? What were you thinking? I can't believe that you would betray me like this. I got you the job here. You turn around, become a whistleblower, and call the press to share company secrets."

"Wait a minute. What the hell are you talking about? I didn't tell the press anything. They have been calling me and asking questions about the business deals with

Tedesco and Landrieu. I haven't told them anything. I'm waiting for someone at RIHIP or the agency to tell me what's going on, so I can respond to this reporter."

"Well, someone's lying. An all-employee memo went out early in the week directing everyone to immediately cease any contact with you, regardless of whether it's business or personal. I could get fired just for calling you. Dick told me directly that you called the media and alerted them to the fact that we do business with some of the legislators. And that you shared details that no one but you would know."

"Joan, there's no law against doing business with elected officials in Rhode Island. They are part-time legislators, who work for a living. It just has to be above board. And I didn't call anyone. Between New Jersey and Florida, I'm doing more work than I can handle. Do you think I would take time from growing my business to chase reporters?"

"Well, I agree that it doesn't make sense, but then who would have tipped off the journalist?

"There was probably no tip-off. Tedesco's show is on TV. Anyone could see it and see that it's sponsored by RIHIP. Dick's stupidity and arrogance are what made it into headline news. And as far as the contract with Landrieu, it wouldn't take much to learn about it. Any cursory investigation would uncover all the business dealings the company has with several legislators. In fact, one of the legislators is a broker that gets commissions from RIHIP on insurance sales through your department. And he's one of your friends. Watch out when that story breaks.

"It all points to Nichols getting caught in a compromising situation and throwing it off on me. Well, at least now I know what to say to the reporter when she calls on Monday."

"Dave, don't you dare talk to the press. It's too dangerous."

"Dangerous for who? Dick is trying to throw me under the bus. I've got no choice but to cover my ass, and no one will do it for me. Oh, and thanks for the vote of confidence."

A Brief Statement

At 8 am on Monday morning, the journalist again called Dave. As soon as he answered, she began firing questions at him. He stopped her and said, "I am not going to answer your questions at this time. I will make a brief statement."

"Would it be okay if I record it?"

"I have no problem with that. If you're ready, here goes.

"My name is Dave Powers, and I am the former Chief Communications Officer at Rhode Island Health Insurance Partners. I served in that capacity for five years up until a year and a half ago. As part of my responsibility, I entered into purchasing agreements with Jacques Landrieu and Ken Tedesco. Although I had the authority to execute such contracts without additional approval, both of these agreements were directed to me and overseen by senior executives at RIHIP."

"Can you provide the names of the executives?

"I will not provide names at this time, other than to say that they were at the Executive Vice-President level or higher. And that is all I have to say at this time."

Elisa had come into the office during the call. When he hung up, she asked if he had been taking to the reporter from the Observer.

"Yes, I must have been her first call this morning. I think I have to get a lawyer. This is going to get very hazardous. I'm in over my head and I'll be up against the RIHIP executives and their legal team. And you know they will lie through their teeth."

Chapter 95

The Invitation

Neil Cornel, a prosecutor from the Criminal Division of the US Attorney General's office in Rhode Island called Dave about the Tedesco TV show. He explained that his office had subpoenaed all records from RIHIP relating to Ken Tedesco. As a result of his findings, he was convening a grand jury to hear evidence collected.

He was informally inviting Dave to testify at the hearing. This made Dave nervous, since he had signed the contract with Tedesco. He asked, "Do I need a lawyer for this appearance? And when will it take place?"

The prosecutor responded, "The grand jury convenes two weeks from Monday, and you are scheduled for that Thursday. RIHIP has engaged an attorney for you. I would recommend that you meet with this attorney before testifying, but of course, he will not be present in the jury room with you."

The following day, Dave got a registered letter from RIHIP's corporate counsel, telling him that they had engaged, at company expense, an attorney to represent him. RIHIP would continue to pay all legal fees, unless the discovery or litigation process revealed that Powers had broken the law in any way.

He called the attorney, Richard Schendel and got a call back that afternoon. Schendel told Dave that he just received the evidence package and had not a chance to review it. He told Dave to plan on meeting him at his office on Westminster Street on Wednesday morning at 10, the day before his testimony. He also said he would call back if he uncovered anything of concern from the evidence package.

The call left Dave apprehensive. Schendel was all business and gave no indication about how this was going to go.

Is this guy Cornell going to try to implicate me in this TV show deal? I'm certain Nichols is going to try to create some evidence to make me look guilty. I don't trust that bastard.

Chapter 96

The Star Witness

The Providence Biltmore is a landmark that is rich in history. Anyone of any importance who ever visited this historic city has roomed at this near century's old hotel. Dave stayed at the iconic facility as the guest of the US Attorney General. They also covered his flight, meals and expenses for the three-day stay in order for him to testify before the grand jury.

On his first morning there, he met with Richard Schendel. Rick as he liked to be called was a solid, beefy guy, who played semi-pro hockey and had the same demeanor as a seasoned defenseman. It turned out that he was also a former prosecutor at the US Attorney's office in Rhode Island, and he had known Neil Cornell for several years.

He explained the grand jury process to Dave and told him in no uncertain terms that he was to answer only the questions asked. At no time should he offer any opinions or stray from the exact response.

"Yes or no is always the best answer. No explanations are necessary unless you are probed for additional information. Witnesses always get in trouble when they start to wander and offer comment that they think the prosecutor is looking for. The prosecutor has a very specific agenda. He therefore builds on seemingly meaningless trivia and then gets to the damning evidence. Follow his lead, and you will be just fine. Do you understand what I'm telling you?"

"Yes. I get it. I have testified in court before, although not in a grand jury setting."

"Dave you are on your own in there. If you get in trouble, you can always ask for a recess to speak to your attorney. I will be sitting right outside the door.

"Now here's what I know about your appearance. The RIHIP executives have already testified that they were unaware of this TV show and its sponsorship by RIHIP. They claim that as a maverick executive, you decided on your own to work with Tedesco and produce the show."

"Wait a minute. That's not true. I wrote a memo back then that I prepared on instructions from the CEO Dick Nichols. And I signed the contract with Tedesco under his direct orders."

Interrupting him, Rick said, "I know. When the FBI seized all Tedesco's records, and fortunately, he kept copious notes, they contained all the details. He originally presented his concept to Philip Lyons, and within a week Lyons told him it was approved. The details also show that you went to Tedesco's office at the statehouse and signed the contract. No one else from RIHIP attended. I think that's where Nichols and friends think they can pin this on you. However, the FBI just uncovered your memo in RIHIP's archives that shows you strongly recommended rejecting the proposal." He then handed Dave a copy of the memo.

Dave responded, "That's my note, which they told me to delete from my computer and destroy any paper copies."

"The investigating team also noted that the document was not in the archives after the first day, meaning it had been deleted following the first night's system backup.

"And that's what the prosecutor will lead up to as he interrogates you in that jury room. So, keep your eye on the prize, because before he gets you to that point, he may take you in other directions. He will build up to the payoff, and you will end up being the star witness that slams the door on the case."

The testimony went exactly as Rick had described. Cornell was a badgering questioner, and he kept Dave off balance. And at the right time he brought down the curtain by presenting the memo, which Dave acknowledged that he wrote. And when asked, he confirmed that he was ordered to delete it from his files. And with that Dave was dismissed.

Dave flew home feeling like a rock star. *Now that I've been through one, I'm sure they will be calling me to testify in the Landrieu scam. I would savor the opportunity to bury Lyons and Nichols.*

Chapter 97

Trials and Tribulations

Back home, Dave began to read the Rhode Island Observer online. And about a month after he returned, a headline article appeared that announced that Kenneth Tedesco had pleaded guilty to multiple charges of bribery and extortion with companies doing business with the State. And he was sentenced to seven to ten years in prison. The promising career of another Rhode Island politician, this one with visions of becoming governor, had been destroyed by greed and poor judgment.

Dave noted that the article made no mention of the grand jury or how it factored in the guilty plea. He called Schendel to learn more.

And Rick explained, "Since no indictment was handed down, the transcripts were sealed. But the evidence presented was so overwhelming that had the case gone to trial Tedesco would have gotten an even longer sentence. He made the wise choice after hearing the mountain of data compiled against him to make the plea. And he made the deal before the grand jury completed its work. Tedesco knew he was toast and decided to plead a deal."

Dave also asked about the Landrieu investigation. After the original story in the press, that episode seemed to have disappeared.

Rick responded, "Trust me Dave. That one is still very much alive. The director of the FBI's New England branch, Edward Beau Davidson has delayed his announced retirement until this investigation is complete. There are now several Rhode Island legislators under the microscope and a few of them have ties to RIHIP. Rhode Island is a cesspool when it comes to corruption, particularly at the local and state level. And the people here simply accept it as part of the fabric of life. They keep reelecting these guys, even after they serve their time."

Chapter 98

Another Invitation

With their branding and marketing consultation service continuing to grow in New Jersey and Sarasota, Dave and Elisa split their time between their two locations. It involved a lot of expensive travel time, but the perks of having a home in a resort destination made it all worthwhile.

About a year after his Tedesco testimony, Dave got a heads-up call from Rick Schendel. The US Attorney's office was moving forward with the prosecution of Landrieu and assembling a grand jury. Rick told him to expect a call from Cornell's office requesting that he testify.

Having put Rhode Island out of his mind in the interim, Dave again began to read The Observer online. However, there was no mention of Landrieu being a target. The one small article he read was that there was an ongoing investigation of legislators, and indictments would be forthcoming.

Nothing occurred for another two months, and then he got a call from an administrative staff person at the Attorney General's office. She advised him that he was being called to appear. Her task was to confirm dates and arrange transportation and lodging. She allowed for a day to consult with his attorney, a day for the pre-testimony conference with the prosecutor and the FBI chief, and a half day for the grand jury appearance. Since the airport was only 20 minutes from downtown, she had him on an afternoon return flight to arrive in Sarasota about seven on that same day as his grand jury appearance.

Chapter 99

A Person of Interest

On his way to the airport, Dave got a text from Schendel telling him to come directly to his office for their conference. The prosecutor wanted to see them that day, rather than the following morning. Apparently, the FBI investigator had a lot of questions for him. Rick mentioned he would have lunch ready when Dave arrived.

Dave's flight was late, so by the time he got to Rick's office, there was no opportunity to prep him for his interview with the FBI. As he wolfed down a sandwich, Rick repeated the same response protocol that he explained the last time he testified. After that, they walked the two blocks to the Rhode Island offices of the Attorney General. As they made their way, Dave seemed excited and enthusiastic about the meeting with the FBI chief. Rick cautioned him by saying, "This is serious, so change your attitude."

Dave responded, "How many people ever get to be interrogated by the FBI? This is going to be more fun than the last investigation."

"In my profession, I know hundreds, and none of them liked being in front of a tough agent. Trust me, when you leave that room, you will not feel like you had fun. These people play hardball, so you had better be sharp."

"But I'm their star witness. Last time they treated me like a celebrity."

"Dave, this is different. This time you're not a witness, but a person of interest. And I don't know why they gave you that designation, but to me it is a significant concern. The one thing I know is that Steve Fisher, Landrieu's partner, claims he never met you, even though his name is on all the documents that you signed requesting bag purchases. I just don't know how it all fits. So be very careful. And keep in mind that Beau Davidson is not your friend. He'll come on like a warm southern gentleman, but he's the best interrogator I've ever met."

Chapter 100

The Grilling

At that point, they arrived at the federal building and went up to Neil Cornell's office. They were shown into a small conference room and asked to have a seat. A few minutes later Cornell and Davidson came in through another door and introductions were made.

As they sat back down, both Cornell and Schendel took out their yellow legal pads to take notes.

In any new situation, Dave was always compelled to lighten the atmosphere with his brand of humor. And this stiff, stodgy setting called for a comment. "So, is this going to be a good-cop, bad-cop scenario? I was expecting to be taken into an interrogation room with a one-way mirror, chained to a desk and grilled for hours."

Rick exhaled uncomfortably but said nothing. Beau Davidson was the first to speak. And with a smile, he ignored Dave's comment and explained to him that the purpose of the meeting was to get all the facts straight. "Mr. Powers, the last thing we want to do is to get you into that jury room and be surprised by an answer we weren't expecting. Now, if you don't mind, I would like to walk through the process of how y'all came about doing business with House Leader Landrieu. And all the details of the working relationship, to the best that your memory can recall."

Davidson then began the questioning by asking Dave to state his name, address, position when he worked at RIHIP, and when he left the company. During these perfunctory questions, Beau told an anecdote about one of his friends from Georgia who worked for RIHIP during the time Dave was employed there. The name did not register.

When questioned about how he met Landrieu, he responded that it was through a request from Phil Lyons, the company's VP of Legislative Affairs. Lyons originally sent him an email, and then came to his office, telling him that Landrieu had a proposal and requested an opportunity to meet with him to evaluate the offer.

Beau then asked, "Mr. Powers, would you mind telling me where the meeting took place, and who attended?"

The question reminded Dave about Rick's comment that Fisher claimed he never met Dave. That had been gnawing at him since he mentioned it. And Dave could not understand why Steve had made that claim. Dave concluded that Steve Fisher was hiding something. He answered the question by stating the original meeting was held in Dave's office at RIHIP and was attended by Jack Landrieu and his associate Steve Fisher."

Cornell immediately looked up and asked, "Are you telling us that Steve Fisher attended that meeting in your office? Are you sure about that?"

"Absolutely. They came together, although Landrieu did all the talking. They both gave me their business cards. And Jack explained that Fisher would be the contact person for all orders and follow-up."

"Fisher was in your office? What was the date of that meeting?"

"Neil, that was six years ago. I really can't remember the exact date. You have copies of all my files when I worked there. It should certainly be on my calendar."

Davidson stepped in and said, "Let's move on. We can check that date later.

"How long after the initial meeting did you place the first order with their company? And how was the order placed?"

"We placed the order within a few weeks of the initial meeting. My production manager handled the project directly with Steve Fisher. I did not participate in that aspect of the production."

Again, Cornell jumped up, "Did Steve Fisher come to RIHIP's office to get the order?"

"I don't really know. I wasn't involved with the handoff of the first order. It may have been done over the phone, and the print files sent via email. But I would have expected that Fisher came to the office for the initial order." Dave deliberately added the last comment, as he was really baffled by this denial of ever meeting him. As he said it, he could see Rick turning to him as a signal not to expand his answers.

For the next two hours, Beau Davidson went over every detail of every order that was placed with Landrieu. And he inquired about what ongoing role Lyons played in the process.

After walking them through the process of Landrieu managing the inventory and requesting purchase orders when they were running out of stock. RIHIP was one of the country's leading insurers for these policies.

The company was therefore convinced that the marketing effort was working well.

Dave told Beau that after the initial introduction, Lyons was not directly involved in the program. However, a year or two later when Dave's department was transferred to Legislative Affairs, Lyons got more personally involved and took charge of the project himself.

"Mr. Powers, I noticed that at one point the orders began to increase, and over a period of time that increase was substantial. Was this when Lyons became involved?"

"Yes, I believe that timing coincided. Lyons was not familiar with the ongoing projects my department produced, but he was engaged in that program. As I explained before, Lyons brought the original proposal to me. And I'm sure Landrieu was telling him of the prescription bag program's success."

Neil Cornell interrupted the proceedings at that point and said, "Gentlemen, we have to end this session at this time, but there is much more to go through. Can we meet again at 9:30 tomorrow morning?"

Rick responded in the affirmative, and they left the building. They walked back to his office so Dave could pick up his suitcase. On the way, Rick expressed his concern about Fisher. Neither of them could understand why Fisher insisted that he never met Dave. Schendler asked Dave, "Based on his reaction during your questioning, Fisher is a sore spot with Cornell. Are you sure that you met Steve Fisher, and that he came to your office?"

"Absolutely. He was not a memorable guy, and at this point, I couldn't tell you what he looked like but the two of them definitely came together to my office for that first meeting."

Dave opted to walk to the Holiday Inn, rather than have Rick call him a cab. He thought the fresh air would help clear his head so he could analyze the interview. Unlike the meeting when he prepped for the Tedesco jury testimony, this was more of an interrogation than an interview. Cornell's entire attitude was noticeably different, much more adversarial. Even the fact that on this trip they booked him into the Holiday Inn, rather than the opulent Biltmore like the last time was not lost on him.

He spent the entire evening trying to unravel Cornell's strategy and end game. And he just couldn't come up with an answer. This caused him a stress-filled sleepless night.

Chapter 101

Drilling Down

They arrived at Cornell's office at 9:30 promptly. Dave was anxious to get the meeting over with as quickly as possible. The intense questioning during this interview was making him uncomfortable and had him a little off balance. He had also made plans for a late lunch with some of his former RIHIP staff.

Neil Cornell displayed his usual grumpy demeanor, while Beau Davidson addressed Dave with his drippy southern charm. "Mr. Powers, I trust y'all had a good night's sleep in our beautiful city. What fine restaurant did you choose for your dinner?" After Dave responded that he slept well and had dinner at Angelo's Civita Farnese, Beau ignored his answer and moved right onto the interrogation.

"This morning I have some questions about the order processing and inventory control for these paper bags. Would you be so kind as to take me through the steps in placing an order?"

"Following the first order, the purchasing was a fairly simple set of steps. Steve Fisher would contact my production manager, Denise Moran and advise her that the inventory was running down. She would write a requisition for me to sign and send it to the Purchasing Department for the PO to be cut and sent to Fisher."

"Where were these bags stored? A million bags seem like a lot of material. How long did it take to use that many?"

"The arrangement we had was that the prescription bags were stored at the manufacturer and drop shipped directly to the independent pharmacies as they requested them. One order of a million bags usually lasted about six months."

"And David, what was the approval process for paying your vendors for printing, such as these bags?"

"We had a solid system of checks and balances for payment processing. In fact, I was instrumental in getting that process organized." As he said that, Dave could again feel Rick turning to him in silent objection to the added comment. Shrugging off the distraction, Dave continued to explain the details of the method.

Thinking ahead, Dave realized that Davidson was setting him up for a question that he couldn't answer. And then it came. "So, David, did the bag company get signed receipts from the pharmacists when they shipped bags to them? Did you have copies of those shipping documents in the packages of paperwork that you used for payment?"

"This program was different from any other printing project. All printing orders are shipped RIHIP's warehouse, but in this case, the material never went to the warehouse, so we didn't have that paper trail."

That response brought the sleeping bear to life. Cornell had been busy taking notes, but he jumped on that opening and Dave knew it was coming. "Are you telling us that you had no documentation that these prescription bags were delivered, and yet you approved the invoices for payment? You just described the process you set up for payment, and yet you violated it for dozens of orders over a five-year period for this one vendor. Were there other vendors that were allowed to get paid without proof of delivery?"

"Not that I know of. This was the only vendor that warehoused and drop shipped product for RIHIP, so their processing did not fit our protocol."

"But how do you know they delivered the tens of millions of bags? It seems impossible that there were that many prescriptions written by a small number of pharmacies."

"We had thank-you letters from some of the pharmacies, so we knew they received them. And with 100,000 seniors picking up multiple prescriptions for maintenance drugs each month, 10 million bags is not a stretch. If they all shopped the independents, that would come to about three or four hundred thousand a month." Dave felt good about being able to justify the quantity, but he knew he was vulnerable on the delivery question.

"Mr. Powers, do you have much experience buying printing?"

"Sir, earlier in my career, I was a printing broker, contracting out printing assignments for my clients. Over the years, I have purchased millions of dollars in printing."

Davidson, at that point changed topics and reminded Dave, "Yesterday you said that you met Steve Fisher at your office when they first pitched the paper bag program. Was there any other time you met him?"

Quickly thinking, Dave could not remember a specific instance where they met, but he answered, "I'm quite certain he came to the office a few times to meet with Denise, and I'm pretty sure we had the opportunity to say hello and shake hands."

"Did you ever meet Fisher outside the office, say at lunch or some function?"

"We had a vendor fair in one of the ballrooms at the Biltmore, and I have a recollection that he came to that function." Dave was freelancing here, as he could not ever remember meeting Steve other than the original meeting with Landrieu. But, because Fisher claimed that they never met, Dave decided to put that lie to rest. In Dave's mind, Fisher's denial meant that he was hiding something, and was therefore shifting the focus to him. Maybe this was the reason he had become a person of interest.

"Are you positive he was at that vendor affair?"

"No, I can't be absolutely certain, but I'm quite sure he stopped in that evening. Every company in the state was there trying to get business or increase their share of orders from us."

"And you are positive you met him at the office from time to time?"

Again, I can't swear to specific occurrences, but I'm sure I ran into him a few times at RIHIP."

Davidson resumed his questioning, and asked, "During the time you were doing business with Mr. Landrieu through your employer, did you have any other business dealings with him outside the firm? Did you have any kind of personal relationship with him?"

Realizing the bullet he had dodged when he opted not to accept Jack's offer to help with the golf course development, Dave answered, "Other than the bag program for RIHIP, I had no other business dealings with Mr. Landrieu. Socially, I met him for lunch once or twice, and played golf at his country club on one occasion."

And who paid for those social events?"

"In all cases Mr. Landrieu paid."

At that point Neil spoke up and announced that it was time for lunch. He suggested they meet back in the same conference room in one hour. Dave was disappointed at this development, as he would now have to cancel lunch with his staff. But before they left the conference room, Neil sternly addressed Dave, "Powers, before you return to this room after lunch, I want you to think long and hard about the answers you gave. And I want you to be certain beyond any doubt that every response is completely accurate. If you have to change any answers, you need to do that this afternoon. Tomorrow it will be too late, because perjury in court is a serious issue." With that, he picked up his pad and papers and rushed out of the room.

Chapter 102

A Lunch Break

Dave and Rick went into a small restaurant on Weybosset Street and ordered sandwiches. When they sat down, Rick said, "Dave I don't like how this interview is going. We should have been done yesterday, and now it looks like you'll be answering questions the rest of the day. You are scheduled for testimony tomorrow morning, which doesn't leave much time to resolve the conflict in Cornell's mind. His last comment to you is very unlike something he would say. Is there something you are hiding from me? If you've done something wrong, I need to know. Otherwise, I can't protect you. Did you do anything illegal with Landrieu, anything at all?"

"Absolutely not! I am an honest, ethical guy. I would never do anything against the law. And I don't have anything to hide. I've done nothing wrong here. This prescription bag program was an excellent promotion at a bargain price, and we kept it going for over five years. If Landrieu was providing special favors for RIHIP as a result of this program, that's between him and Lyons. In fact, when Lyons took it over from me, he increased the quantities and the frequency. Maybe that's when he and Landrieu were doing a deal. I was completely out of the process by then."

"There's something going on that they haven't told us yet. We'll find out this afternoon because you appear at the grand jury hearing tomorrow morning."

"Rick, I still don't understand why Fisher denied ever meeting me. Does he know something? It would make sense if he were aware that Lyons and Landrieu were working on some kind of bribery deal. He could be distancing himself from any wrongdoing. But if there was something going on, I wasn't part of it, and I wasn't aware of it. I will swear to it."

"OK, OK. I believe you. Let's get back to the interview and find out what's missing from this equation."

Chapter 103

Grilling After Lunch

When they reconvened, Beau Davidson had his usual broad smile, while Neil Cornell wore his best scowl. Neil, put his pen down, took off his glasses and addressed Dave. "Mr. Powers, I hope you took the time to review your responses to our questions and have some different answers from this morning's questioning."

"I'm sorry Mr. Cornell, but I don't. I answered every question honestly and to the best of my ability. I also qualified a few answers by saying that I wasn't positive about particular points, given that they took place several years ago."

"Then let me advise you about certain evidence we hold, and maybe that will change your mind." With that, Rick turned to Dave with a questioning look. Neil continued, "RIHIP placed 15 orders over about a five-year period, for paper bags at a cost of well over $600,000. And no bags, not one, were ever delivered to any of the pharmacies. The bag manufacturer produced a proof run of 100 sample bags to be approved for production, but no approval was ever provided. And so, no bags were ever produced. Now what do you have to say, Mr. Powers?"

Dave sat there stunned. He couldn't believe this was true. His mind was racing, trying to find an answer that would refute Cornell's claim. But every objection, every detail had a plausible explanation. The one delivery of the hundred samples was Landrieu's solution to pull off the caper. He provided some of them for approval before production. And he attached copies to his invoices as support for completion of each order.

Dave recognized that Landrieu could have easily created phony thank you letters. And he realized that somehow, he knew about the flaw in the accounts payable processing system. Without the bag shipments going into RIHIP's warehouse, the AP department would never know that the bags had not been produced. But Landrieu could only know that with inside help. Other than Purchasing staff, his own production team, and Phil Lyons, no one knew the accounts payable protocol. Therefore, Lyons was definitely working a deal with Jack Landrieu.

"Neil, I don't have an answer for you. I cannot believe that I was duped so easily, and this elected official could scam one of the largest companies in the state."

"I also find it incomprehensible, particularly when you were the person being duped after describing your extensive background in purchasing printing.

"I also recognize that Landrieu could not have executed this scam without your help. He had no way of knowing the elaborate system of payment processing that you installed in the company unless you told him about it and how to beat it.

"Mr. Powers, we know you colluded with Jack Landrieu to scam the Rhode Island Health Insurance Partners out of over a half a million dollars. But you're not the target here. We are not interested in putting you in jail. For you, the statute of limitations has expired on this theft. But if you go into that courtroom tomorrow and testify before the grand jury by telling these lies, we will prosecute you for perjury. So now I want you to tell us the details of this embezzlement, so we can convict Landrieu of these crimes."

While Cornell spoke, Dave sat there turning white. This was the last thing he was expecting. He came up to Rhode Island to be the star witness, just like with the Tedesco trial. And now, he's being accused of fraud and threatened with jail. This can't be happening.

Faltering, he responded in barely above a whisper to Cornell's request. "I have no details to give you. I did not participate in this elaborate fraud. I got duped, and professionally I am totally embarrassed about it.

"But there is no way that I would ever get involved in a dishonest or illegal act against my employer, or anyone for that matter. That is a line I would never cross. If you decide that you don't want me to testify tomorrow, I will get on a plane and fly home. But I cannot offer you any information to help convict Landrieu for engineering this fraud."

Cornell was visibly angry. He stood up and said to Dave, "Then this interview is over. Tomorrow morning, I will expect you at the hearing. But tonight, I will again remind you to think over the answers you gave today. There are serious inconsistencies in your testimony, and I will charge you if you lie on that witness stand. Whatever you do, don't take this lightly." And with that, he and Davidson stood to leave the conference room.

Beau gave a disappointed look at Dave, shook his head and they both walked out.

Back on the street the street, Rick asked Dave, "I'm missing something here. There's more to this than I'm seeing. What do you know that you haven't told me? Remember I had his job, so I know how he's thinking. There's some contradiction in your statements and responses that just don't fit, and it must be important. Tonight, I want you to think about every answer you gave and determine what might be hurting his case. I will review my notes and do the same. Let's meet in front of the courthouse at 8:30 tomorrow morning and walk through this one more time. You are in serious trouble, so we have got to figure this out."

Dave walked back to the hotel in a daze. He felt limp and his shirt was soaked with perspiration.

I can't fathom all the conflicting facts about this interrogation, but there is something I don't know that is putting me in an impossible position. It must be about Lyons or Fischer. All I know is that I could end up going to jail.

Chapter 104

The Threat

The next morning Rick and Dave were sitting on a bench in the hallway of the US District Court Building reviewing Dave's responses of the last two days. Rick commented, "I went through all my notes and there is nothing I can see that is of any consequence in your upcoming testimony. Did you recall anything that could come back to bite you?"

Dave confirmed his finding. He had thought about everything he said over the last two days and there wasn't anything that stood out. His only reservation was the answers about having met Fisher. But even then, he qualified them by saying that he was not totally certain they met, other than that first appointment. It was the only possible flaw he did not share with Rick.

Cornell and Davidson came into the courthouse with a third gentleman, acknowledged them and went directly into the prosecutor's anteroom. A few minutes later the three of them came out, walked up to Rick and Dave, and asked them to follow. The five men entered a small conference room that was being used more as a storage space than a meeting room. In addition to the table and six chairs, the room was cluttered with AV equipment and displays from previous hearings.

They sat around the crowded table and Neil spoke. First, he introduced Albert Regni, the Deputy Attorney General saying, "Just so you understand, the Deputy Attorney General just flew in from Washington to oversee this portion of the grand jury testimony. This is a critically important case, and we want to be sure that this hearing proceeds without any inaccurate testimony.

"Mr. Powers, have you reviewed your answers to our questions, and do you wish to share any changes in the testimony you will give this morning?"

"I did go over everything I said to you during the last two days, and there's nothing to change."

"Mr. Powers," It was Regni addressing Dave, "I believe that Mr. Cornell has explained to you that you are in no danger of prosecution in this case, but if you are not truthful in that jury room, I have instructed him to prosecute you for perjury without leniency."

Neil then spoke, "Look Powers, you have been evasive and dishonest in our interviews. We have irrefutable evidence that you have been lying to us."

With that, Dave jumped out of his seat, and shouted, "That's fucking bullshit!" Before he could say more Rick grabbed him and sat him down saying, "Don't say another word."

At that point, the three men stood up and began walking out of the room. A visibly angry Cornell looked down at Dave and spit out, "You've got five minutes to decide if you're going to testify truthfully. And if you don't appear in that hearing, I will find a way to charge you in this case."

When they left the room, Rick was red with anger. He turned to Dave and said, "Now you have to tell me what you know that is in conflict with your testimony. They are not playing games here. This is that serious that they will charge you with something."

"Rick, there is no reason for me to be dishonest with you. I don't know what they are looking for, but right now I am scared shitless. It must have something to do with Fisher. But I don't what else to say about him."

Dave was now pacing and continued, "Let me share something unrelated and maybe you'll understand me better. When I was eleven, I sold firecrackers to my classmates in New York City. That was technically illegal, not that the police would prosecute me, but every time the doorbell rang, I thought they were coming to arrest me. That terrorizing experience was so indelible, I swore back then I would never break the law again. It was not worth the stress that I suffered. I had a chance to do something illegal with Landrieu, a personal project with an unbelievable payoff, ten times the value of this bag shit, but I walked way."

Rick nodded, "Okay, you wait here. I'll be right back." He then left the room and went to the prosecutor's office and used his relationship with Cornell to try to resolve the matter.

The twenty-five minutes that it took Rick to discuss the issue with Cornell seemed like a lifetime to Dave, sitting alone in that tiny claustrophobic conference room. He got up and began to pace alongside the table, but when he looked up at one of the dust-covered TV monitors, his growing paranoia convinced him that it contained a surveillance camera, and they were watching him. He quickly sat down and assumed a posture of confidence, while he sweated internally. His fear was exacerbated by the fact that he had no control over what was about to happen to him. He could not think of what he could truthfully change in his testimony to satisfy Cornell.

The thought again struck him about the golf course project.

If I had made a deal with Jack Landrieu and arranged that kickback, I would be going to prison. They are out for blood.

Finally, Rick returned and shared what he learned. "Steve Fisher is the star witness in this case, and it goes far beyond the RIHIP prescription bag debacle. Apparently, Landrieu was scamming other companies, and was also using his firm to launder bribe money from people seeking political favors. Fisher was worried that he would be caught up in the scheme and decided to become a witness instead of a defendant.

"Fisher has already testified to the grand jury that he has never met you. He did not attend any meetings at RIHIP. So, Landrieu must have brought along someone to impersonate Fisher to the meeting. Cornell thinks that he used a surrogate, so the purchase orders would be addressed to Fisher instead of him.

"And now you understand the predicament you were creating for Cornell, and how your testimony could destroy the case."

Beginning to feel some relief, Dave commented, "Well, now it all makes sense. And it explains why Fisher never met me. But why didn't they tell us that at the beginning?"

"Dave, both Davidson and Cornell were convinced that you were in on the deal. Therefore, unless you confessed or cooperated, they were going to find a way to make you pay for your part in the crime. With the statute of limitations passed, they would have destroyed your reputation if they couldn't find a way to prosecute you.

"You somehow made them believe you, even when I was beginning to have doubts. They are going to focus their full attention on Lyons and Nichols. They have some evidence from the RIHIP archives, and they plan to exploit that to their advantage.

"Now here's the new plan of action that I just worked out with Neil. He is going to interrogate you on the stand and, ask you about your background and career experience. You will testify about the referral from Phil Lyons, and the subsequent orders for the bags. And through his questioning, he will show how you were duped, and how someone else at RIHIP helped engineer this scam. That will support his other witnesses and contribute to his getting the indictment.

"And remember! He's the orchestra leader. Even if you don't agree with the way he's handling the questions, answer them simply and honestly. I told him that you were very good at thinking on your feet. You would follow his train of thought and answer accordingly. He may ask some open-ended questions, so in this case it's OK to expand your answers. Just keep his goal in mind. Now, let's go. It's your turn at bat."

Chapter 105

Grand Jury Testimony

A reassured Dave walked into the jury room feeling confident and composed. As he sat on the witness stand, he looked around, expecting to see a box along the wall with the typical 12 jurors. Instead, the middle of the room was filled with at least 20 people seated behind rows of narrow tables. They all looked attentive and curious. Neil Cornell sat at a small table to the side.

After Dave was sworn in, Cornell got up and began with the usual name, rank and serial number questions for the record, and then went into Dave's credentials and areas of expertise. Neil then requested details of his bio and work history. He asked Dave about how he got the job at RIHIP, his responsibilities and his record of performance. Then, more specifically, he queried, "Tell us more about your role at the company."

"Operationally, I led the effort to reorganize the print procurement process with a new multi-step protocol that allowed us the freedom of vendor selection and protected the company from erroneous or inaccurate billing."

Neil then questioned him further on the purchasing program to learn more about the specifics of the process.

Dave was enjoying this portion of the interrogation, as it made him out to be an experienced, executive, recognized for his innovation and results.

By the time Neil finished building up his background and performance, it was time for the lunch break. Once again, Dave was disappointed in the amount of time spent with the questioning. He had expected to be done by now and getting ready for his flight back home.

When he exited the jury room, Rick was seated at a bench across from doorway. With him was a woman that looked familiar. As he approached, he recognized her as Cornell's assistant. She told him that she had cancelled his return flight and was booking him a seat on a flight later in the day. She would have his ticket ready when he returned from lunch.

Rick and Dave walked back to the same restaurant they ate at the day before and Rick began his questions. But first he said, "You look a lot better than you did when you walked into the jury room. Did it go OK?"

"It actually went better than you described. All of a sudden, he's my new best friend."

"He's not your friend. You are a tool in his quest to convict a crook. He will do whatever he has to, in order to get the indictment and ultimately win this case. Were you careful about expanding your answers, as I advised you?"

"For the most part, yes. But he did ask some open-ended questions about my awards and performance reviews, so I did elaborate some. But even then, I didn't carry on and give him a speech."

"That's OK. Just remember to stay alert. This afternoon is when the hammer comes down. And it's going to come down hard. He's going to lead you into the answers that will seal Landrieu's fate."

Chapter 106

The Climax

Dave took his seat on the witness stand, and Neil reminded him that he was still under oath. He resumed the interrogation by recapping to the jurors Dave's impressive background and then said, "We will now talk about Mr. Powers' business relationship with House Leader Jacques Landrieu. Sir, how did you come about knowing this legislator?"

"I received an email from Mr. Phil Lyons, Vice President of Legislative Affairs at RIHIP asking me to meet with Mr. Landrieu because he had a proposal that he wanted to present to us. Landrieu then came to my office to discuss the project in more detail."

"Tell us about the meeting. What was the proposal all about?"

Dave proceeded to explain the offer for producing the prescription bags. He outlined the cost and the value proposition, which encouraged him to accept the proposal. When asked if Landrieu came alone, Dave responded, "No, he came with a man he described as his partner, Steve Fisher."

"Why did you say, 'described as his partner'? What does that mean?"

"The man was introduced as Landrieu's partner, but I have since learned that he was an imposter. Steve Fisher never came to my office."

"So, you dealt with Landrieu directly?"

"As per his instructions, we addressed and forwarded all purchase orders to Fisher, although I did meet with Landrieu from time to time."

"And how long did the program run?"

"The program ran for over five years. At Lyons direction, I initiated it and managed it for the first year or two. And then Phil Lyons took it over directly when my department was transferred to his division."

"You ran that one program for over five years, Mr. Powers? It must have been very successful."

"Actually, there would have been no way to determine if that specific program was successful. We were running multiple promotions within the Medicare insurance campaign. Our overall sales and marketing effort enabled RIHIP to lead the country in policies sold.

"However, we learned much later that for the entire time we purchased those prescription bags, none were ever delivered."

"So, are you telling this jury that you ordered over 10 million bags over a five-year period, and those bags were never shipped to the pharmacies? And you learned this well after the fact. That is incredulous! How could that be?"

"It was a bold scam perpetrated by the house leader to defraud RIHIP.

"But Mr. Powers, you explained your lengthy career, with expertise in purchasing printing. Do you expect us to believe that you could be duped for such a long period of time?"

Cornell put him on the spot with that question and Dave's ego was crushed as he fumbled with his answer, "As embarrassing as it is, I did get fooled. And there is no excuse for that. Had we not been running so many other programs simultaneously we could have measured the results of the bag promotion and realized it was a scam.

"And since I only controlled the program for less than two years when Lyons took it over, I was not aware of how it kept expanding."

"Ten million bags, Mr. Powers. Didn't you ever think to confirm that any of them were delivered? Did you just go on blind faith?"

Again, struggling to answer, Dave, in a little more than a whisper responded, "Mr. Cornell, one of my character flaws is that I trust people, and it takes a lot to break that trust. I was doing business with who I considered to be one of Rhode Island's leading citizens." He heard snickers from the jurors with that statement, and Cornell turned and glared at them.

Continuing he said, "This was a grave miscalculation on my part, and it is something I will carry with me forever."

"But this wasn't a simple theft. There must be more to this elaborate caper. Earlier you boasted about installing a foolproof system to prevent this very thing from happening. How did all those invoices get paid if the product wasn't delivered?"

"The Achilles' heel is this process was exposed when shipments were not delivered to RIHIP's warehouse. And because it was standard practice to store material in the warehouse, we had no way to confirm delivery to any other destinations. In order for the scam to work, Landrieu had to know the approval process for paying bills, had to know about this flaw to bypass the checks and balances. Someone at RIHIP must have been helping him with that information."

"Do you think it was someone in Purchasing?"

"I doubt it. I knew all of them and they were dedicated and beyond reproach."

"Was there anyone else at the company who had knowledge of this system, and motive to help Landrieu? Had you told anyone about the process?"

"The initial order for the bags occurred very shortly after we put the purchase protocol in place. Therefore, very few people in the entire organization knew about the change in ordering. However, about that same time, Phil Lyons came to my office, something he never did, and asked about purchasing promotional gifts for legislators and their staff. Lyons insisted on making his own selections and doing his own purchasing. Since he was referring to very small dollar amounts, and he was a vice president, I didn't contest his request. And he was the only company employee that I ever told about the process."

Turning to the jury, Neil instructed them as he thumbed through his own paperwork, "Please open your evidence binders to page 146." And he brought a printed sheet up to the witness stand and asked Dave to read it. It was a copy of an email from Lyons to Nichols and a handwritten note from Nichols in response at the bottom. The contents read:

To: Richard Nichols, President and CEO
From: Philip Lyons, VP Legislative Affairs
The transfer of the communications department from Sales & Marketing to Legislative Affairs was completed without issue. I was surprised that neither Joan Rotino nor Dave Powers

registered a complaint since his department's responsibilities are way outside the scope of Legislative Affairs.

But now that it is complete, I can take over any programs that we want to keep under the radar.

Good work Phil,

I knew Powers would fall into line without a fight. I was more concerned about Rotino. She can be a real bitch when you mess with her people.

Keep track of the money, so I know how much JL is into us for. This way I know how hard I can squeeze him.

D.

"Mr. Powers, have you seen this memo before? And can you vouch for its authenticity?"

"I never saw the memo before, but I'm certainly aware of the transfer of my department to Legislative Affairs. And this document appears to explain why it took place when there was no logical reason for it.

"Regarding the authenticity, the fact that there is a handwritten note from Nichols at the bottom only adds to its credibility. You see, Dick Nichols never learned to use a computer, so his secretary would print all his emails and he would then dictate responses, or sometimes write notes in reply. She then emailed the responses or delivered the hand-written ones. So, this literally has Nichols' fingerprints on it."

The prosecutor's office had a cab waiting for Dave as he exited the federal courthouse late that afternoon. He arrived at Green Airport in 25 minutes with less than a half hour to make his flight.

Racing to the gate he was the last person to board. Relieved, he slumped in his seat and reflected on his emotional day. Dave was one of those people who rarely suffered from stress. He used humor to defuse difficult situations and made every task a fun experience. But as much as he tried, he could find no way to enjoy these arduous days of interrogation.

And even today, Cornell, after building up his image, had made him look like a totally incompetent fool. And that made it so difficult for Dave to recover. He had always been proud of his integrity and work ethic, and even more so about his creativity, performance, and knowledge. Despite the understanding of Neil's strategy to make Dave's testimony more believable, it did not assuage his battered feelings and self-esteem.

The only comfort he drew from this encounter was that Lyons, and probably Nichols would go down with Landrieu over this brazen embezzlement. The memo, although vague was a smoking gun that tied the loose ends together.

Epilogue

After being indicted by the Grand Jury, Jack Landrieu went on trial for multiple bribery and embezzlement charges. He was convicted and is currently serving a fifteen-year sentence. His business partner, Steve Fisher was given immunity for testifying against him and not charged. Their company immediately shut down and Steve took a sales position with a large packaging company in Chicago.

Phil Lyons' participation in the prescription bag program, plus his admission to other illegal activities with the legislators resulted in him being indicted for bribery. He pled a deal to serve three years in a minimum-security facility after he agreed to become a witness and testify in Landrieu's trial. However, the conviction and the plea agreement required him to resign from the Rhode Island bar and be banned from ever running for public office again.

Lyons was fortunate to land a position, through a colleague in a large Providence law firm. Since he couldn't practice law, he was relegated to providing research on cases for some of the partners. It was a role he despised after his high-flying career. But he was getting a modest paycheck that was his reward for the many favors he had done for his colleague over his years as a power broker.

###

Having barely survived his involvement in the Tedesco conviction, Dick Nichols was again under fire over the news surrounding RIHIP's participation in Landrieu's embezzlement scheme. And when his exorbitant salary and outlandish perks were made public, health organizations such as the Rhode Island Medical Society began to picket RIHIP's executive headquarters. All of this was too much for his allies on the Board, and despite all his bluster, he had no choice but to resign as CEO of the company.

Unconcerned, he considered the termination a blessing, as he was certain that he could get a much higher paying CEO position with another insurer. He immediately engaged an executive recruiter with extensive experience in the field to place him as head of one of the larger health insurance companies. Taking all the credit for the company's turnaround, despite it happening at the end of Al Conover's watch, he was convinced any insurer in the country would want him.

After six months without one interview, Dick decided to investigate other industries. His love of exotic cars drove him to seek an opportunity in that field. He then hired a headhunter in the automotive industry. The results were no better there.

Since his first wife got his entire retirement package in their settlement, he was rapidly running out of money as he always spent every cent he earned, he was having trouble making payments on his six-bedroom, custom home overlooking Narragansett Bay. But the good news from Dick's perspective was that his golf game was really improving. After all, he now played every day. Although this was probably the reason that his second wife Louise abruptly left him and filed for divorce.

Prior to the divorce, they had put their house up for sale. However, the only prospects that came to see it were curiosity seekers, but no serious buyers. After eight months and three price reductions, there was not one offer. The rumor that circulated through the real estate community was that the house was tainted with the ghost of Nichols' arrogance. When it finally sold, they barely made a profit and Louise got half of that.

Andy Westbrook, the company's COO was named interim President. He inherited a mess with all the publicity surrounding the Tedesco and Landrieu trials, and the problems showed up quickly. Several of the major clients and many of the smaller companies cancelled their group policies, forcing large layoffs within RIHIP for the first time in its history.

Everything Andy knew about the company he had learned from Dick Nichols through his private tutelage when Andy joined the firm. He used that knowledge as he cleaned house and pared the staff. Because of his role in the bribery schemes, Phil Lyons had been dismissed immediately upon the announcement of his guilty verdict. Just about all the remaining VPs were the weakest ones who had posed no threat to Dick.

Joan Rotino survived the cut and attempted to cozy up to Andy with her vivacious personality, but they were like oil and water. He never met a joke that he liked. And he was convinced that if he ever smiled, his face would break. At lunch one day with a manager from Operations, Joan shared her frustration with Andy, complaining that he didn't understand her or appreciate her value to the company. Here sales ability was the only way the company could survive. Joan was also sure Andy wouldn't last long at the company. Her caustic comments got back to him. The next morning, an HR manager and two security guards came to Joan's office, terminated her and escorted her out to the parking lot.

And so, the restructured company was left with feckless management and clueless leadership. It quickly became a minor player in the Rhode Island insurance market.

As RIHIP shrunk, Bruce Dane picked off most of the talent in the communications department, adding them to his staff. He ultimately lost the RIHIP account, but his agency was able to survive with the addition of several large Boston-based companies, and his firm thrived.

He never opened a Florida office. But instead, he bought a home in St. Martin where he spends his vacations sailing the Caribbean.

Dave Powers and his wife Elisa continued their success in the New Jersey and Sarasota areas, taking on several large accounts in both markets. Their long-term plan was to grow the New Jersey business and sell it while continuing the Sarasota office and eventually moving there full-time.

One day, Dave got an email from an old RIHIP colleague. It contained a link to a YouTube video. When he clicked on the start button, the clip showed Dick Nichols standing in a used car lot, selling a beat-up Toyota Scion to an unsuspecting buyer. Dave mused that Dick traversed the gamut from driving a sleek Mercedes SL Roadster to selling junk cars. Wow!

Their business in New Jersey grew substantially after Dave and Elisa successfully pitched the Dizzy Don's retail appliance store chain.

The account proved to be low maintenance and they both spent time in Sarasota building sales in the region. And then one day a call came from DeeDee that changed their lives forever.

Special Thanks and Acknowledgements

To assist me in getting this previously published novel from the original draft to the updated text and become Book 2 of the Dave Powers Series, I enlisted some members of **The Flash Mob**. These mobsters provided ideas and input for the new cover design and book description. They include Lucy Svagen, Charlie and Linda Shuford, Nick DeSimone, LeeAnn Friend, John Mills, Cindy Brylinsky, Jackie Taeschler, and Cheryl Hacker.

My editor for this book was Andrew Parker who did an excellent job of improving my work and adding more angst and drama to the story.

And if you like to read and like to laugh, learn about our unique group and consider joining. My newsletters and blogs are laugh-out-loud funny and enjoy and unheard-of open rate of up to 70%. And a fraction of 1% ever drop out. See details on the next page.

<u>The Importance of Book Reviews</u>

In addition to my writing, I read about 40 books a year. And I write a review on each one of them. It's that important.

If you like the result of my team's collaboration and enjoyed this book, *please* write a review on Amazon or wherever you purchased this book. All of us who worked on this novel would sincerely appreciate it.

I can't stress enough the importance of readers like you writing reviews for books you enjoy. They have a profound effect on the success of the book.

Simply give it the number of stars you think appropriate and write a few words about how the story affected you.

THE FLASH MOB

The brainchild of multiple award-winning author Michael A. Sisti, this is a growing number of over 700 hundred people including his friends, business associates, social contacts, all avid readers with a diverse age, socio-economic, and educational demographic. The common thread is they all like to read and like to laugh. They are also interested in getting involved in the creative and production of books. And many are interested in writing their own book. So, if you like to read, and want to participate in sharing your opinion on book titles, cover designs, manuscripts, etc., the join the Mob. Use link below to learn more.

"I don't know of any other author that has organized an advisory group of this size. I never feel like I am trapped in a room, staring at a screen, suffering from writer's block. I simply call in the Mob, give away some gifts, and move forward. And the best part is, we're all having fun!"

–Michael A. Sisti

"My firm has published nearly a thousand books for 940 authors with sales of over 900,000 books. While most authors have a fan base, Michael Sisti has a large, dedicated organization. Sisti's first book with us is the product of this synergetic collaboration, and why we signed him. We have great expectations that his entire book series will be extremely successful."

–John Koehler, President, Koehler Books

https://michaelsisti.com/flash-mob

Other Books by Michael A. Sisti

Dave Powers Series

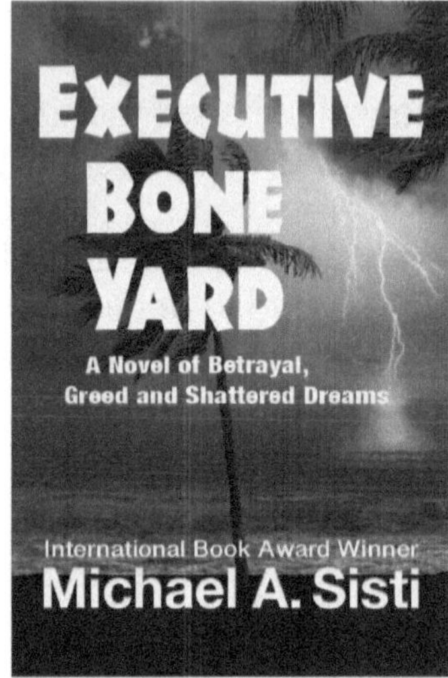

Self Help Book

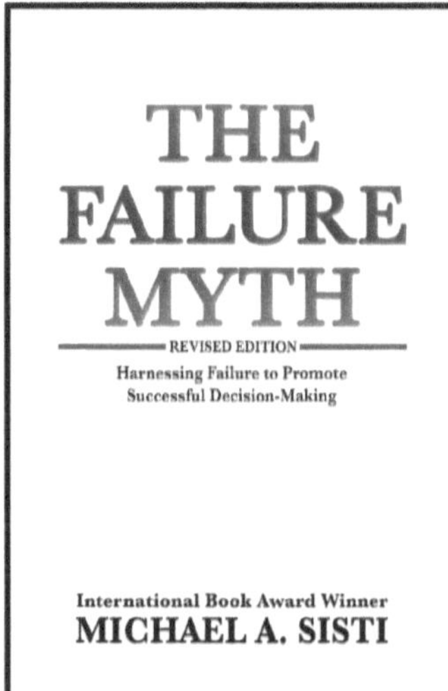

www.michaelsisti.com

Other Books by Michael A. Sisti

The books on this page are being edited and will be republished soon

Dave Powers Series

Humor Series